Spiritual Tales

by Fiona Macleod

(William Sharp)

Originally published in 1897.

To LILAVAN

... For I have seen

In lonely places, and in lonelier hours,

Beyond the involving veils of day and night

Circumfluent o'er the shadowy drift of years,

My vision of the rainbow-aureoled face

Of her whom men name Beauty: proud, austere,

Inviolate, immortal, undismayed

By the swift-eddying dust of wandering Time—

Dim vision of the flawless, perfect Face,

Divinely fugitive, that haunts the world

And lifts man's spiral thought to lovelier dreams.

SPIRITUAL TALES

"I like to think that these spiritual chronicles might as well, in substance, have been told a thousand years ago or be written a thousand years hence. That Fisher still haunts the invisible shadowy stream of human tears; those mystic Spinners still ply their triple shuttles, and the fair Weaver of Hope now as of yore and for ever sends his rainbows adrift across the hearts and through the minds of men.... These tales, let me add, are not legendary mysteries but legendary moralities. They are reflections from the mirror that is often obscured but is never dimmed. There is no mystery in them, or anywhere; except the eternal mystery of beauty." (From the Prologue to The Washer of the Ford.)

CONTENTS

NOTE

The tales in this volume which have not hitherto appeared are "The Melancholy of Ulad" and "The Hills of Ruel." "The Awakening of Angus Ogue" is also for the first time printed in book form, though it appeared in the Winter number of The Evergreen. Of the re-issued stories "The Anointed Man" is from The Sin-Eater, and the others are from The Washer of the Ford. As these tales have not been re-set, they are, except in the matter of pagination and re-arrangement, necessarily unaltered.

ST. BRIDE OF THE ISLES

NOTE

This legendary romance is based upon the ancient and still current (though often contradictory) legends concerning Brighid, or Bride, commonly known as "Muime Chriosd"—i.e. the Foster-Mother of Christ. From the universal honour and reverence in which she was and is held—second only in this respect to the Virgin herself— she is also called "Mary of the Gael." Another name, frequent in the West, is "Brighde-nam-Brat"—i.e. St Bride of the Mantle, a name explained in the course of my legendary story. Brighid the Christian saint should not, however, be confused with a much earlier and remoter Brighid, the ancient Celtic Muse of Song.

SLOINNEADH BRIGHDE, MUIME CHRIOSD

Brighde nighean Dughaill Duinn,

'Ic Aoidth, 'ic Arta, 'ic Cuinn.

Gach la is gach oidhche

Ni mi cuimhneachadh air sloinneadh Brighde.

Cha mharbhar mi,

Cha ghuinear mi,

Cha ghonar mi,

Cha mho dh' fhagas Criosd an dearmad mi;

Cha loisg teine gniomh Shatain mi;

'S cha bhath uisge no saile mi;

'S mi fo chomraig Naoimh Moire

'S mo chaomh mhuime, Brighde.

The Genealogy of St Bridget or St Bride, Foster-Mother of
Christ

St Bridget, the daughter of Dùghall Donn,

Son of Hugh, son of Art, son of Conn.

Each day and each night

I will meditate on the genealogy of St Bridget.

[Whereby] I will not be killed,

I will not be wounded,

I will not be bewitched;

Neither will Christ forsake me;

Satan's fire will not burn me;

Neither water nor sea shall drown me;

For I am under the protection of the Virgin Mary,

And my gentle foster-mother, St Bridget.

I

Before ever St Colum came across the Moyle to the island of Iona, that was then by strangers called Innis-nan-Dhruidhneach, the Isle of the Druids, and by the natives Ioua, there lived upon the south-east slope of Dun-I a poor herdsman named Dùvach. Poor he was, for sure, though it was not for this reason that he could not win back to Ireland, green Banba, as he called it: but because he was an exile thence, and might never again smell the heather blowing over Sliabh-Gorm in what of old was the realm of Aoimag.

He was a prince in his own land, though none on Iona save the Arch-Druid knew what his name was. The high priest, however, knew that Dùvach was the royal Dùghall, called Dùghall Donn, the son of Hugh the King, the son of Art, the son of Conn. In his youth he had been accused of having done a wrong against a noble maiden of the blood. When her child was born he was made to swear across her dead body that he would be true to the daughter for whom she had given up her life, that he would rear her in a holy place, but away from Eiré, and that he would never set foot within that land again. This was a bitter thing for Dùghall Donn to do: the more so as, before the King, and the priests, and the people, he swore by the Wind, and by the Moon, and by the Sun, that he was guiltless of the thing of which he was accused. There were many there who believed him because of that sacred oath: others, too, forasmuch as that Morna the Princess had herself sworn to the same effect. Moreover, there was Aodh of the Golden Hair, a poet and seer, who avowed that Morna had given birth to an immortal, whose name would one day be as a moon among the stars for glory. But the King would not be appeased, though he spared the life of his youngest son. So it was that, by the advice of Aodh of the Druids, Dùghall Donn went northwards through the realm of Clanadon and so to the sea-loch that was then called Loc Feobal. There he took boat with some wayfarers bound for Alba. But in the Moyle a tempest arose, and the frail galley was driven northward, and at sunrise was cast like a fish, spent and dead, upon the south end of Ioua, that is now Iona. Only two of the mariners survived: Dùghall Donn and the little child. This was at the place where, on a day of the days in a year that was not yet come, St Colum landed in his coracle, and gave thanks on his bended knees.

When, warmed by the sun, they rose, they found themselves in a waste place. Ill was Dùghall in his mind because of the portents, and now to his fear and amaze the child Bridget knelt on the stones, and, with claspt hands, small and pink as the sea-shells round about her, sang a song of words which were unknown to him. This was the more marvellous, as she was yet but an infant, and could say no word even of Erse, the only tongue she had heard.

At this portent, he knew that Aodh had spoken seeingly. Truly this child was not of human parentage. So he, too, kneeled, and, bowing before her, asked if she were of the race of the Tuatha de Danann, or of the older gods, and what her will was, that he might be her servant. Then it was that the kneeling babe looked at him, and sang in a low sweet voice in Erse:

I am but a little child,

Dùghall, son of Hugh, son of Art,

But my garment shall be laid

On the lord of the world,

Yea, surely it shall be that He

The King of the Elements Himself

Shall lean against my bosom,

And I will give him peace,

And peace will I give to all who ask

Because of this mighty Prince,

And because of his Mother that is the Daughter of Peace.

And while Dùghall Donn was still marvelling at this thing, the Arch-Druid of Iona approached, with his white-robed priests. A grave welcome was given to the stranger. While the youngest of the servants of God was entrusted with the child, the Arch-Druid took Dùghall aside and questioned him. It was not till the third day that the old man gave his decision. Dùghall Donn was to abide on Iona if he so willed: but the child was to stay. His life would be spared, nor would he be a bondager of any kind, and a little land to till would be given him, and all that he might need. But of his past he was to say no word. His name was to become as nought, and he was to be known simply as Dùvach. The child, too, was to be named Bride, for that was the way the name Bridget was called in the Erse of the Isles.

To the question of Dùghall, that was thenceforth Dùvach, as to why he laid so great stress on the child that was a girl, and the reputed offspring of shame at that, Cathal the Arch-Druid replied thus: "My kinsman Aodh of the Golden Hair who sent you here, was wiser than Hugh the King and all the Druids of Aoimag. Truly, this child is an Immortal. There is an ancient prophecy concerning her: surely of her who is now here, and no other. There shall be, it says, a spotless maid born of a virgin of the ancient immemorial race in Innisfail. And when for the seventh time the sacred year has come, she will hold Eternity in her lap as a white flower. Her maiden breasts shall swell with milk for the Prince of the World. She shall give suck to the King of the Elements. So I say unto you, Dùvach, go in peace. Take unto thyself a wife, and live upon the place I will give thee on the east side of Ioua. Treat Bride as though she were thy spirit, but leave her much alone, and let her learn of the sun and the wind. In the fulness of time the prophecy shall be fulfilled."

So was it, from that day of the days. Dùvach took a wife unto himself, who weaned the little Bride, who grew in beauty and grace, so that all men marvelled. Year by year for seven years the wife of Dùvach bore him a son, and these grew apace in strength, so that by the beginning of the third year of the seventh cycle of Bride's life there were three stalwart youths to brother her, and three comely and strong lads, and one young boy fair to see. Nor did anyone, not even Bride herself, saving Cathal the Arch-Druid, know that Dùvach the herdsman was Dùghall Donn, of a princely race in Innisfail.

In the end, too, Dùvach came to think that he had dreamed, or at the least that Cathal had not interpreted the prophecy aright. For though Bride was of exceeding beauty, and of a strange piety that made the young Druids bow before her as though she were a bàndia, yet the world went on as before, and the days brought no change. Often, while she was still a child, he had questioned her about the words she had said as a babe, but she had no memory of them. Once, in her ninth year, he came upon her on the hillside of Dun-I singing these self-same words. Her eyes dreamed far away. He bowed his head, and, praying to the Giver of Light, hurried to Cathal. The old man bade him speak no more to the child concerning the mysteries.

Bride lived the hours of her days upon the slopes of Dun-I, herding the sheep, or in following the kye upon the green hillocks and grassy dunes of what then as now was called the Machar. The beauty of the world was her daily food.

The spirit within her was like sunlight behind a white flower. The birdeens in the green bushes sang for joy when they saw her blue eyes. The tender prayers that were in her heart for all the beasts and birds, for helpless children, and tired women, and for all who were old, were often seen flying above her head in the form of white doves of sunshine.

But when the middle of the year came that was, though Dùvach had forgotten it, the year of the prophecy, his eldest son, Conn, who was now a man, murmured against the virginity of Bride, because of her beauty and because a chieftain of the mainland was eager to wed her. "I shall wed Bride or raid Ioua," was the message he had sent.

So one day, before the great fire of the summer-festival, Conn and his brothers reproached Bride.

"Idle are these pure eyes, O Bride, not to be as lamps at thy marriage-bed."

"Truly, it is not by the eyes that we live," replied the maiden gently, while to their fear and amazement she passed her hand before her face and let them see that the sockets were empty.

Trembling with awe at this portent, Dùvach intervened.

"By the Sun I swear it, O Bride, that thou shalt marry whomsoever thou wilt and none other, and when thou willest, or not at all if such be thy will."

And when he had spoken, Bride smiled, and passed her hand before her face again, and all there were abashed because of the blue light as of morning that was in her shining eyes.

II

The still weather had come, and all the isles lay in beauty. Far south, beyond vision, ranged the coasts of Eiré: westward, leagues of quiet ocean dreamed into unsailed wastes whose waves at last laved the shores of Tir-ná'n-Òg, the Land of Eternal Youth: northward, the spell-bound waters sparkled in the sunlight, broken here and there by purple shadows, that were the isles of Staffa and Ulva, Lunga and the isles of the columns, misty Coll, and Tiree that is the land beneath the wave; with, pale blue in the heat-haze, the mountains of Rûm called Haleval, Haskeval, and Oreval, and the sheer Scuir-na-Gillian and the peaks of the Cuchullins in remote Skye.

All the sweet loveliness of a late spring remained, to give a freshness to the glory of summer. The birds had song to them still.

It was while the dew was yet wet on the grass that Bride came out of her father's house, and went up the steep slope of Dun-I. The crying of the ewes and lambs at the pastures came plaintively against the dawn. The lowing of the kye arose from the sandy hollows by the shore, or from the meadows on the lower slopes. Through the whole island went a rapid trickling sound, most sweet to hear: the myriad voices of twittering birds, from the dotterel in the sea-weed to the larks climbing the blue spirals of heaven.

This was the morning of her birth, and she was clad in white. About her waist was a girdle of the sacred rowan, the feathery green leaves of it flickering dusky shadows upon her robe as she moved. The light upon her yellow hair was as when morning wakes, laughing low with joy amid the tall corn. As she went she sang, soft as the crooning of a dove. If any had been there to hear he would have been abashed, for the words were not in Erse, and the eyes of the beautiful girl were as those of one in a vision.

When, at last, a brief while before sunrise, she reached the summit of the Scuir, that is so small a hill and yet seems so big in Iona where it is the sole peak, she found three young Druids there, ready to tend the sacred fire the moment the sun-rays should kindle it. Each was clad in a white robe, with fillets of oak leaves; and each had a golden armlet. They made a quiet obeisance as she approached. One stepped forward, with a flush in his face because of her beauty, that was as a sea-wave for grace, and a flower for purity, and sunlight for joy, and moonlight for peace, and the wind for fragrance.

"Thou mayst draw near if thou wilt, Bride, daughter of Dùvach," he said, with something of reverence as well as of grave courtesy in his voice: "for the holy Cathal hath said that the Breath of the Source of All is upon thee. It is not lawful for women to be here at this moment, but thou hast the law shining upon thy face and in thine eyes. Hast thou come to pray?"

But at that moment a low cry came from one of his companions. He turned, and rejoined his fellows. Then all three sank upon their knees, and with outstretched arms hailed the rising of God.

As the sun rose, a solemn chant swelled from their lips, ascending as incense through the silent air. The glory of the new day came soundlessly. Peace was in the blue heaven, on the blue-green sea, on the green land. There was no wind, even where the currents of the deep moved in shadowy purple. The sea itself was silent, making no more than a sighing slumber-breath round the white sands of the isle, or a hushed whisper where the tide lifted the long weed that clung to the rocks.

In what strange, mysterious way, Bride did not see; but as the three Druids held their hands before the sacred fire there was a faint crackling, then three thin spirals of blue smoke rose, and soon dusky red and wan yellow tongues of flame moved to and fro. The sacrifice of God was made. Out of the immeasurable heaven He had come, in His golden chariot. Now, in the wonder and mystery of His love, He was re-born upon the world, re-born a little fugitive flame upon a low hill in a remote isle. Great must be His love that He could die thus daily in a thousand places: so great His love that He could give up His own body to daily death, and suffer the holy flame that was in the embers He illumined to be lighted and revered and then scattered to the four quarters of the world.

Bride could bear no longer the mystery of this great love. It moved her to an ecstasy. What tenderness of divine love that could thus redeem the world daily: what long-suffering for all the evil and cruelty done hourly upon the weeping earth: what patience with the bitterness of the blind fates! The beauty of the worship of Be'al was upon her as a golden glory. Her heart leaped to a song that could not be sung. The inexhaustible love and pity in her soul chanted a hymn that was heard of no Druid or mortal anywhere, but was known of the white spirits of Life.

Bowing her head, so that the glad tears fell warm as thunder-rain upon her hands, she rose and moved away.

Not far from the summit of Dun-I is a hidden pool, to this day called the Fountain of Youth. Hitherward she went, as was her wont when upon the hill at the break of day, at noon, or at sundown. Close by the huge boulder, which hides it from above, she heard a pitiful bleating, and soon the healing of her eyes was upon a lamb which had become fixed in a crevice in the rock. On a crag above it stood a falcon, with savage cries, lusting for warm blood. With swift step Bride drew near. There was no hurt to the lambkin as she lifted it in her arms. Soft and warm was it there, as a young babe against the bosom that mothers it. Then with quiet eyes she looked at the falcon, who hooded his cruel gaze.

"There is no wrong in thee, Seobhag," she said gently; "but the law of blood shall not prevail for ever. Let there be peace this morn."

And when she had spoken this word, the wild hawk of the hills flew down upon her shoulder, nor did the heart of the lambkin beat the quicker, while with drowsy eyes it nestled as against its dam. When she stood by the pool she laid the little woolly creature among the fern. Already the bleating of it was sweet against the forlorn heart of a ewe. The falcon rose, circled above her head, and with swift flight sped through the blue air. For a time Bride watched its travelling shadow: when it was itself no more than a speck in the golden haze, she turned, and stooped above the Fountain of Youth.

Beyond it stood then, though for ages past there has been no sign of either, two quicken-trees. Now they were gold-green in the morning light, and the brown-green berries that had not yet reddened were still small. Fair to see was the flickering of the long finger-shadows upon the granite rocks and boulders.

Often had Bride dreamed through their foliage; but now she stared in amaze. She had put her lips to the water, and had started back because she had seen, beyond her own image, that of a woman so beautiful that her soul was troubled within her, and had cried its inaudible cry, worshipping. When, trembling, she had glanced again, there was none beside herself. Yet what had happened? For, as she stared at the quicken-trees, she saw that their boughs had interlaced, and that they now became a green arch. What was stranger still was that the rowan-clusters hung in blood-red masses, although the late heats were yet a long way off.

Bride rose, her body quivering because of the cool sweet draught of the Fountain of Youth, so that almost she imagined the water was for her that day what it could be once in each year to every person who came to it, a breath of new life and the strength and joy of youth. With slow steps she advanced towards the arch of the quickens. Her heart beat as she saw that the branches at the summit had formed themselves into the shape of a wreath or crown, and that the scarlet berries dropped therefrom a steady rain of red drops as of blood. A sigh of joy breathed from her lips when, deep among the red and green, she saw the white merle of which the ancient poets sang, and heard the exceeding wonder of its rapture, which was now the pain of joy and now the joy of pain.

The song of the mystic bird grew wilder and more sweet as she drew near. For a brief while she hesitated. Then, as a white dove drifted slow before her under and through the quicken-boughs, a dove white as snow but radiant with sunfire, she moved forward to follow, with a dream-smile upon her face and her eyes full of the sheen of wonder and mystery, as shadowy waters flooded with moonshine.

And this was the passing of Bride, who was not seen again of Dùvach or her foster-brothers for the space of a year and a day. Only Cathal, the aged Arch-Druid, who died seven days thence, had a vision of her, and wept for joy.

III

When the strain of the white merle ceased, though it had seemed to her scarce longer than the vanishing song of the swallow on the wing, Bride saw that the evening was come. Through the violet glooms of dusk she moved soundlessly, save for the crispling of her feet among the hot sands. Far as she could see to right or left there were hollows and ridges of sand; where, here and there, trees or shrubs grew out of the parched soil, they were strange to her. She had heard the Druids speak of the sunlands in a remote, nigh unreachable East, where there were trees called palms, trees in a perpetual sunflood yet that perished not, also tall dark cypresses, black-green as the holy yew. These were the trees she now saw. Did she dream, she wondered? Far down in her mind was some memory, some floating vision only, mayhap, of a small green isle far among the northern seas. Voices, words, faces, familiar yet unfamiliar when she strove to bring them near, haunted her.

The heat brooded upon the land. The sigh of the parched earth was "Water, water."

As she moved onward through the gloaming she descried white walls beyond her: white walls and square white buildings, looming ghostly through the dark, yet home-sweet as the bells of the cows on the sea-pastures, because of the yellow lights every here and there agleam.

A tall figure moved towards her, clad in white, even as those figures which haunted her unremembering memory. When he drew near she gave a low cry of joy. The face of her father was sweet to her.

"Where will be the pitcher, Brighid?" he said, though the words were not the words that were near her when she was alone. Nevertheless she knew them, and the same manner of words was upon her lips.

"My pitcher, father?"

"Ah, dreamer, when will you be taking heed! It is leaving your pitcher you will be, and by the Well of the Camels, no doubt: though little matter will that be, since there is now no water, and the drought is heavy upon the land. But ... Brighid...."

"Yes, my father?"

"Sure now, it is not safe for you to be on the desert at night. Wild beasts come out of the darkness, and there are robbers and wild men who lurk in the shadow. Brighid ... Brighid ... is it dreaming you are still?"

"I was dreaming of a cool green isle in northern seas, where...."

"Where you have never been, foolish lass, and are never like to be. Sure, if any wayfarer were to come upon us you would scarce be able to tell him that yonder village is Bethlehem, and that I am Dùghall Donn the innkeeper, Dùghall, the son of Hugh, son of Art, son of Conn. Well, well, I am growing old, and they say that the old see wonders. But I do not wish to see this wonder, that my daughter Brighid forgets her own town, and the good inn that is there, and the strong sweet ale that is cool against the thirst of the weary. Sure, if the day of my days is near it is near. 'Green be the place of my rest,' I cry, even as Oisìn the son of Fionn of the hero-line of Trenmor cried in his old age; though if Oisìn and the Fiànn were here not a green place would they find now, for the land is burned dry as the heather after a hill-fire. But now, Brighid, let us go back into Bethlehem, for I have that for the saying which must be said at once."

In silence the twain walked through the gloaming that was already the mirk, till they came to the white gate, where the asses and camels breathed wearily in the sultry darkness, with dry tongues moving round parched mouths. Thence they fared through narrow streets, where a few white-robed Hebrews and sons of the desert moved silently, or sat in niches. Finally, they came to a great yard, where more than a score of camels lay huddled and growling in their sleep. Beyond this was the inn, which was known to all the patrons and friends of Dùghall Donn as the "Rest and Be Thankful," though formerly as the Rest of Clan-Ailpean, for was he not himself through his mother MacAlpine of the Isles, as well as blood-kin to the great Cormac the Ard-Righ, to whom his father, Hugh, was feudatory prince?

As Dùghall and Bride walked along the stone flags of a passage leading to the inner rooms, he stopped and drew her attention to the water-tanks.

"Look you, my lass," he said sorrowfully, "of these tanks and barrels nearly all are empty. Soon there will be no water whatever, which is an evil thing though I whisper it in peace, to the Stones be it said. Now, already the folk who come here murmur. No man can drink ale all day long, and those wayfarers who want to wash the dust of their journey from their feet and hands complain bitterly. And ... what is that you will be saying? The kye? Ay, sure, there is the kye; but the poor beasts are o'ercome with the heat, and there's not a Cailliach on the hills who could win a drop more of milk from them than we squeeze out of their udders now, and that only with rune after rune till all the throats of the milking lassies are as dry as the salt grass by the sea.

"Well, what I am saying is this: 'tis months now since any rain will be falling, and every crock of water has been for the treasuring as though it had been the honey of Moy-Mell itself. The moon has been full twice since we had the good water brought from the mountain-springs; and now they are for drying up too. The seers say that the drought will last. If that is a true word, and there be no rain till the winter comes, there will be no inn in Bethlehem called 'The Rest and Be Thankful'; for already there is not enough good water to give peace even to your little thirst, my birdeen.

As for the ale, it is poor drink now for man or maid, and as for the camels and asses, poor beasts, they don't understand the drinking of it."

"That is true, father; but what is to be done?"

"That's what I will be telling you, my lintie. Now, I have been told by an oganach out of Jerusalem, that lives in another place close by the great town, that there is a quenchless well of pure water, cold as the sea with a north wind in it, on a hill there called the Mount of Olives. Now, it is to that hill I will be going. I am for taking all the camels and all the horses, and all the asses, and will lade each with a burthen of water-skins, and come back home again with water enough to last us till the drought breaks."

That was all that was said that night. But at the dawn the inn was busy, and all the folk in Bethlehem were up to see the going abroad of Dùghall Donn and Ronald McIan, his shepherd, and some Macleans and Maccallums that were then in that place. It was a fair sight to see as they went forth through the white gate that is called the Gate of Nazareth. A piper walked first, playing the Gathering of the Swords: then came Dùghall Donn on a camel, and McIan on a horse, and the herdsmen on asses, and then there were the collies barking for joy.

Before he had gone, Dùghall took Bride out of the hearing of the others. There was only a little stagnant water, he said; and as for the ale, there was no more than a flagon left of what was good. This flagon and the one jar of pure water he left with her. On no account was she to give a drop to any wayfarer, no matter how urgent he might be; for he, Dùghall, could not say when he would get back, and he did not want to find a dead daughter to greet him on his return, let alone there being no maid of the inn to attend to customers. Over and above that, he made her take an oath that she would give no one, no, not even a stranger, accommodation at the inn, during his absence.

Afternoon and night came, and dawn and night again, and yet again. It was on the afternoon of the third day, when even the crickets were dying of thirst, that Bride heard a clanging at the door of the inn.

When she went to the door she saw a weary grey-haired man, dusty and tired. By his side was an ass with drooping head, and on the ass was a woman, young, and of a beauty that was as the cool shadow of green leaves and the cold ripple of running waters. But beautiful as she was it was not this that made Bride start: no, nor the heavy womb that showed the woman was with child. For she remembered her of a dream—it was a dream, sure—when she had looked into a pool on a mountain-side, and seen, beyond her own image, just this fair and beautiful face, the most beautiful that ever man saw since Nais, of the Sons of Usna, beheld Deirdrê in the forest—ay, and lovelier far even than she, the peerless among women.

"Gu'm beannaicheadh Dia an tigh," said the grey-haired man in a weary voice, "the blessing of God on this house."

"Soraidh leat," replied Bride gently, "and upon you likewise."

"Can you give us food and drink, and, after that, good rest at this inn? Sure it is grateful we will be. This is my wife Mary, upon whom is a mystery: and I am Joseph, a carpenter in Arimathea."

"Welcome, and to you, too, Mary: and peace. But there is neither food nor drink here, and my father has bidden me give shelter to none who comes here against his return."

The carpenter sighed, but the fair woman on the ass turned her shadowy eyes upon Bride, so that the maiden trembled with joy and fear.

"And is it forgetting me you will be, Brighid-Alona," she murmured, in the good sweet Gaelic of the Isles; and the voice of her was like the rustle of leaves when a soft rain is falling in a wood.

"Sure, I remember," Bride whispered, filled with deep awe. Then without a word she turned, and beckoned them to follow: which, having left the ass by the doorway, they did.

"Here is all the ale that I have," she said, as she gave the flagon to Joseph: "and here, Mary, is all the water that there is. Little there is, but it is you that are welcome to it."

Then, when they had quenched their thirst she brought out oatcakes and scones and brown bread, and would fain have added milk, but there was none.

"Go to the byre, Brighid," said Mary, "and the first of the kye shall give milk."

So Bride went, but returned saying that the creature would not give milk without a sian or song, and that her throat was too dry to sing.

"Say this sian," said Mary:

Give up thy milk to her who calls

Across the low green hills of Heaven

And stream-cool meads of Paradise!

And sure enough, when Bride did this, the milk came: and
she soothed her thirst, and went back to her guests
rejoicing. It was sorrow to her not to let them stay where
they were, but she could not, because of her oath.

The man Joseph was weary, and said he was too tired to
seek far that night, and asked if there was no empty byre or
stable where he and Mary could sleep till morning. At that,
Bride was glad: for she knew there was a clean cool stable
close to the byre where her kye were: and thereto she led
them, and returned with peace at her heart.

When she was in the inn again, she was afraid once more:
for lo, though Mary and Joseph had drunken deep of the jar
and the flagon, each was now full as it had been. Of the
food, too, none seemed to have been taken, though she had
herself seen them break the scones and the oatcakes.

It was dusk when her reverie was broken by the sound of
the pipes. Soon thereafter Dùghall Donn and his following
rode up to the inn, and all were glad because of the cool
water, and the grapes, and the green fruits of the earth, that
they brought with them.

While her father was eating and drinking, merry because of
the ale that was still in the flagon, Bride told him of the
wayfarers. Even as she spoke, he made a sign of silence,
because of a strange, unwonted sound that he heard.

"What will that be meaning?" he asked, in a low, hushed
voice.

"Sure it is the rain at last, father. That is a glad thing. The earth will be green again. The beasts will not perish. Hark, I hear the noise of it coming down from the hills as well." But Dùghall sat brooding.

"Ay," he said at last, "is it not foretold that the Prince of the World is to be born in this land, during a heavy falling of rain, after a long drought? And who is for knowing that Bethlehem is not the place, and that this is not the night of the day of the days? Brighid, Brighid, the woman Mary must be the mother of the Prince, who is to save all mankind out of evil and pain and death!"

And with that he rose and beckoned to her to follow. They took a lantern, and made their way through the drowsing camels and asses and horses, and past the byres where the kye lowed gently, and so to the stable.

"Sure that is a bright light they are having," Dùghall muttered uneasily; for, truly, it was as though the shed were a shell filled with the fires of sunrise.

Lightly they pushed back the door. When they saw what they saw they fell upon their knees. Mary sat with her heavenly beauty upon her like sunshine on a dusk land: in her lap, a Babe, laughing sweet and low.

Never had they seen a Child so fair. He was as though wrought of light.

"Who is it?" murmured Dùghall Donn, of Joseph, who stood near, with rapt eyes.

"It is the Prince of Peace."

And with that Mary smiled, and the Child slept.

"Brighid, my sister dear"—and, as she whispered this, Mary held the little one to Bride.

The fair girl took the Babe in her arms, and covered it with her mantle. Therefore it is that she is known to this day as Brighde-nam-Brat, St Bride of the Mantle.

And all through that night, while the mother slept, Bride nursed the Child with tender hands and croodling crooning songs. And this was one of the songs that she sang:

Ah, Baby Christ, so dear to me,

Sang Bridget Bride:

How sweet thou art,

My baby dear,

Heart of my heart!

Heavy her body was with thee,

Mary, beloved of One in Three,

Sang Bridget Bride—

Mary, who bore thee, little lad:

But light her heart was, light and glad

With God's love clad.

Sit on my knee,

Sang Bridget Bride:

Sit here

O Baby dear,

Close to my heart, my heart:

For I thy foster-mother am,

My helpless lamb!

O have no fear,

Sang good St Bride.

None, none,

No fear have I:

So let me cling

Close to thy side

Whilst thou dost sing,

O Bridget Bride!

My Lord, my Prince I sing:

My baby dear, my King!

Sang Bridget Bride.

It was on this night that, far away in Iona, the Arch-Druid
Cathal died. But before the breath went from him he had
his vision of joy, and his last words were:

Brighde 'dol air a glùn,

Righ nan dùl a shuidh 'na h-uchd!

(Bridget Bride upon her knee,

The King of the Elements asleep on her breast!)

At the coming of dawn Mary awoke, and took the Child.
She kissed Bride upon the brows, and said this thing to her:
"Brighid, my sister dear, thou shalt be known unto all time
as Muime Chriosd."

IV

No sooner had Mary spoken than Bride fell into a deep
sleep. So profound was this slumber that when Dùghall
Donn came to see to the wayfarers, and to tell them that the
milk and the porridge were ready for the breaking of their
fast, he could get no word of her at all. She lay in the clean,
yellow straw beneath the manger, where Mary had laid the
Child. Dùghall stared in amaze. There was no sign of the

mother, nor of the Babe that was the Prince of Peace, nor of the douce, quiet man that was Joseph the carpenter. As for Bride, she not only slept so sound that no word of his fell against her ears, but she gave him awe. For as he looked at her he saw that she was surrounded by a glowing light. Something in his heart shaped itself into a prayer, and he knelt beside her, sobbing low. When he rose, it was in peace. Mayhap an angel had comforted his soul in its dark shadowy haunt of his body.

It was late when Bride awoke, though she did not open her eyes, but lay dreaming. For long she thought she was in Tir-Tairngire, the Land of Promise, or wandering on the honey-sweet plain of Magh-Mell; for the wind of dreamland brought exquisite odours to her, and in her ears was a most marvellous sweet singing.

All round her there was a music of rejoicing. Voices, lovelier than any she had ever heard, resounded; glad voices full of praise and joy. There was a pleasant tumult of harps and trumpets, and as from across blue hills and over calm water came the sound of the bagpipes. She listened with tears. Loud and glad were the pipes at times, full of triumph, as when the heroes of old marched with Cuculain or went down to battle with Fionn: again, they were low and sweet, like humming of bees when the heather is heavy with the honey-ooze. The songs and wild music of the angels lulled her into peace: for a time no thought of the woman Mary came to her, nor of the Child that was her foster-child.

Suddenly it was in her mind as though the pipes played the chant that is called the "Aoibhneas a Shlighe," "the joy of his way," a march played before a bridegroom going to his bride.

Out of this glad music came a solitary voice, like a child singing on the hillside.

"The way of wonder shall be thine, O Brighid-Naomha!"

This was what the child-voice sang. Then it was as though all the harpers of the west were playing "air clàrsach": and the song of a multitude of voices was this:

"Blessed art thou, O Brighid, who nursed the King of the Elements in thy bosom: blessed thou, the Virgin Sister of the Virgin Mother, for unto all time thou shalt be called Muime Chriosd, the Foster-Mother of Jesus that is the Christ."

With that, Bride remembered all, and opened her eyes. Nought strange was there to see, save that she lay in the stable. Then as she noted that the gloaming had come, she wondered at the soft light that prevailed in the shed, though no lamp or candle burned there. In her ears, too, still lingered a wild and beautiful music.

It was strange. Was it all a dream, she pondered. But even as she thought thus, she saw half of her mantle lying upon the straw in the manger. Much she marvelled at this, but when she took the garment in her hand she wondered more. For though it was no more than a half of the poor mantle wherewith she had wrapped the Babe, it was all wrought with mystic gold lines and with precious stones more glorious than ever Arch-Druid or Island Prince had seen. The marvel gave her awe at last, when, as she placed the garment upon her shoulder, it covered her completely.

She knew now that she had not dreamed, and that a miracle was done. So with gladness she went out of the stable, and into the inn. Dùghall Donn was amazed when he saw her, and then rejoiced exceedingly.

"Why are you so merry, my father," she asked.

"Sure it is glad that I am. For now the folk will be laughing the wrong way. This very morning I was so pleased with the pleasure, that while the pot was boiling on the peats I went out and told every one I met that the Prince of Peace was come, and had just been born in the stable behind the 'Rest and Be Thankful.' Well, that saying was just like a weasel among the rabbits, only it was an old toothless weasel: for all Bethlehem mocked me, some with jeers, some with hard words, and some with threats. Sure, I cursed them right and left. No, not for all my cursing—and by the blood of my fathers, I spared no man among them, wishing them sword and fire, the black plague and the grey death—would they believe. So back it was that I came, and going through the inn I am come to the stable. 'Sorrow is on me like a grey mist,' said Oisìn, mourning for Oscur, and sure it was a grey mist that was on me when not a sign of man, woman, or child was to be seen, and you so sound asleep that a March gale in the Moyle wouldn't have roused you. Well, I went back, and told this thing, and all the people in Bethlehem mocked at me. And the Elders of the People came at last, and put a fine upon me: and condemned me to pay three barrels of good ale, and a sack of meal, and three thin chains of gold, each three yards long: and this for causing a false rumour, and still more for making a laughing-stock of the good folk of Bethlehem. There was a man called Murdoch-Dhu, who is the chief smith in Nazareth, and it's him I'm thinking will have laughed the Elders into doing this hard thing."

It was then that Bride was aware of a marvel upon her, for she blew an incantation off the palm of her hand, and by that frith she knew where the dues were to be found.

"By what I see in the air that is blown off the palm of my hand, father, I bid you go into the cellar of the inn. There you will find three barrels full of good ale, and beside them a sack of meal, and the sack is tied with three chains of gold, each three yards long."

But while Dùghall Donn went away rejoicing, and found that which Bride had foretold, she passed out into the street. None saw her in the gloaming, or as she went towards the Gate of the East. When she passed by the Lazar-house she took her mantle off her back and laid it in the place of offerings. All the jewels and fine gold passed into invisible birds with healing wings: and these birds flew about the heads of the sick all night, so that at dawn every one arose, with no ill upon him, and went on his way rejoicing. As each went out of Bethlehem that morning of the mornings he found a clean white robe and new sandals at the first mile; and, at the second, food and cool water; and, at the third, a gold piece and a staff.

The guard that was at the Eastern Gate did not hail Bride. All the gaze of him was upon a company of strange men, shepherd-kings, who said they had come out of the East led by a star. They carried rare gifts with them when they first came to Bethlehem: but no man knew whence they came, what they wanted, or whither they went.

For a time Bride walked along the road that leads to Nazareth. There was fear in her gentle heart when she heard the howling of hyenas down in the dark hollows, and she was glad when the moon came out and shone quietly upon her.

In the moonlight she saw that there were steps in the dew before her. She could see the black print of feet in the silver sheen on the wet grass, for it was on a grassy hill that she now walked, though a day ago every leaf and sheath there had lain brown and withered. The footprints she followed were those of a woman and of a child.

All night through she tracked those wandering feet in the dew. They were always fresh before her, and led her away from the villages, and also where no wild beasts prowled through the gloom. There was no weariness upon her, though often she wondered when she should see the fair wondrous face she sought. Behind her also were footsteps in the dew, though she knew nothing of them. They were those of the Following Love. And this was the Lorgadh-Brighde of which men speak to this day: the Quest of the holy St Bride.

All night she walked; now upon the high slopes of a hill. Never once did she have a glimpse of any figure in the moonlight, though the steps in the dew before her were newly made, and none lay in the glisten a short way ahead.

Suddenly she stopped. There were no more footprints. Eagerly she looked before her. On a hill beyond the valley beneath her she saw the gleaming of yellow stars. These were the lights of a city. "Behold, it is Jerusalem," she murmured, awe-struck, for she had never seen the great town.

Sweet was the breath of the wind that stirred among the olives on the mount where she stood. It had the smell of heather, and she could hear the rustle of it among the bracken on a hill close by.

"Truly, this must be the Mount of Olives," she whispered, "The Mount of which I have heard my father speak, and that must be the hill called Calvary."

But even as she gazed marvelling, she sighed with new wonder; for now she saw that the yellow stars were as the twinkling of the fires of the sun along the crest of a hill that is set in the east. There was a living joy in the dawntide. In her ears was a sweet sound of the bleating of ewes and lambs. From the hollows in the shadows came the swift singing rush of the flowing tide. Faint cries of the herring gulls filled the air; from the weedy boulders by the sea the skuas called wailingly.

Bewildered, she stood intent. If only she could see the footprints again, she thought. Whither should she turn, whither go? At her feet was a yellow flower. She stooped and plucked it.

"Tell me, O little sun-flower, which way shall I be going?" and as she spoke a small golden bee flew up from the heart of it, and up the hill to the left of her. So it is that from that day the dandelion is called am-Bèarnàn-Bhrighde.

Still she hesitated. Then a sea-bird flew by her with a loud whistling cry.

"Tell me, O eisireùn," she called, "which way shall I be going?"

And at this the eisireùn swerved in its flight, and followed the golden bee, crying, "This way, O Bride, Bride, Bride,

Bride, Bri-i-i-ide!"

So it is that from that day the oyster-catcher has been called the Gille-Bhrighde, the Servant of St Bridget.

Then it was that Bride said this sian:

Dia romham;

Moire am dheaghuidh;

'S am Mac a thug Righ nan Dul!

Mis' air do shlios, a Dhia,

Is Dia ma'm luirg.

Mac' 'oire, a's Righ nan Dul,

A shoillseachadh gach ni dheth so,

Le a ghras, mu'm choinneamh.

God before me;

The Virgin Mary after me;

And the Son sent by the King of the Elements.

I am to windward of thee, O God!

And God on my footsteps.

May the Son of Mary, King of the Elements,

Reveal the meaning of each of these things

Before me, through His grace.

And as she ended she saw before her two quicken-trees, of which the boughs were interwrought so that they made an arch. Deep in the green foliage was a white merle that sang a wondrous sweet song. Above it the small branches were twisted into the shape of a wreath or crown, lovely with the sunlit rowan-clusters, from whose scarlet berries red drops as of blood fell.

Before her flew a white dove, all aglow as with golden light. She followed, and passed beneath the quicken arch.

Sweet was the song of the merle, that was then no more; sweet the green shadow of the rowans, that now grew straight as young pines. Sweet the far song in the sky, where the white dove flew against the sun.

Bride looked, and her eyes were glad. Bonnie the blooming of the heather on the slopes of Dun-I. Iona lay green and gold, isled in her blue waters. From the sheiling of Dùvach, her father, rose a thin column of pale blue smoke. The collies, seeing her, barked loudly with welcoming joy.

The bleating of the sheep, the lowing of the kye, the breath of the salt wind from the open sea beyond, the song of the flowing tide in the Sound beneath: dear the homing.

With a strange light in her eyes she moved down through the heather and among the green bracken: white, wonderful, fair to see.

THE THREE MARVELS OF IONA

I. THE FESTIVAL OF THE BIRDS.

II. THE SABBATH OF THE FISHES AND THE FLIES.

III. THE MOON-CHILD.

I

THE FESTIVAL OF THE BIRDS

Before dawn, on the morning of the hundredth Sabbath after Colum the White had made glory to God in Hy, that was theretofore called Ioua and thereafter I-shona and is now Iona, the Saint beheld his own Sleep in a vision.

Much fasting and long pondering over the missals, with their golden and azure and sea-green initials and earth-brown branching letters, had made Colum weary. He had brooded much of late upon the mystery of the living world that was not man's world.

On the eve of that hundredth Sabbath, which was to be a holy festival in Iona, he had talked long with an ancient greybeard out of a remote isle in the north, the wild Isle of the Mountains, where Scathach the Queen hanged the men of Lochlin by their yellow hair.

This man's name was Ardan, and he was of the ancient people. He had come to Hy because of two things.

Maolmòr, the King of the northern Picts, had sent him to learn of Colum what was this god-teaching he had brought out of Eiré: and for himself he had come, with his age upon him, to see what manner of man this Colum was, who had made Ioua, that was "Innis-nan-Dhruidhneach"—the Isle of the Druids—into a place of new worship.

For three hours Ardan and Colum had walked by the sea-shore. Each learned of the other. Ardan bowed his head before the wisdom. Colum knew in his heart that the Druid saw mysteries.

In the first hour they talked of God. Colum spake, and Ardan smiled in his shadowy eyes. "It is for the knowing," he said, when Colum ceased.

"Ay, sure," said the Saint: "and now, O Ardan the wise, is my God thy God?"

But at that Ardan smiled not. He turned the grave, sad eyes of him to the west. With his right hand he pointed to the Sun that was like a great golden flower. "Truly, He is thy God and my God." Colum was silent. Then he said: "Thee and thine, O Ardan, from Maolmòr the Pictish king to the least of thy slaves, shall have a long weariness in Hell. That fiery globe yonder is but the Lamp of the World: and sad is the case of the man who knows not the torch from the torch-bearer."

And in the second hour they talked of Man. Ardan spake, and Colum smiled in his deep, grey eyes.

"It is for laughter that," he said, when Ardan ceased.

"And why will that be, O Colum of Eiré?" said Ardan. Then the smile went out of Colum's grey eyes, and he turned and looked about him.

He beheld, near, a crow, a horse, and a hound.

"These are thy brethren," he said scornfully.

But Ardan answered quietly, "Even so."

The third hour they talked about the beasts of the earth and the fowls of the air.

At the last Ardan said: "The ancient wisdom hath it that these are the souls of men and women that have been, or are to be."

Whereat Colum answered: "The new wisdom, that is old as eternity, declareth that God created all things in love. Therefore are we at one, O Ardan, though we sail to the Isle of Truth from the West and the East. Let there be peace between us."

"Peace," said Ardan.

That eve, Ardan of the Picts sat with the monks of Iona. Colum blessed him and said a saying. Oran of the Songs sang a hymn of beauty. Ardan rose, and put the wine of guests to his lips, and chanted this rune:

O Colum and monks of Christ,

It is peace we are having this night:

Sure, peace is a good thing,

And I am glad with the gladness.

We worship one God,

Though ye call him Dè—

And I say not, O Dia!

But cry Bea'uil!

For it is one faith for man,

And one for the living world,

And no man is wiser than another—

And none knoweth much.

None knoweth a better thing than this:

The Sword, Love, Song, Honour, Sleep.

None knoweth a surer thing than this:

Birth, Sorrow, Pain, Weariness, Death.

Sure, peace is a good thing;

Let us be glad of Peace:

We are not men of the Sword,

But of the Rune and the Wisdom.

I have learned a truth of Colum,

He hath learned of me:

All ye on the morrow shall see

A wonder of the wonders.

The thought is on you, that the Cross

Is known only of you:

Lo, I tell you the birds know it

That are marked with the Sorrow.

Listen to the Birds of Sorrow,

They shall tell you a great Joy:

It is Peace you will be having,

With the Birds.

No more would Ardan say after that, though all besought him.

Many pondered long that night. Oran made a song of mystery. Colum brooded through the dark; but before dawn he slept upon the fern that strewed his cell. At dawn, with waking eyes, and weary, he saw his Sleep in a vision.

It stood grey and wan beside him.

"What art thou, O Spirit?" he said.

"I am thy Sleep, Colum."

"And is it peace?"

"It is peace."

"What wouldest thou?"

"I have wisdom. Thy heart and thy brain were closed. I could not give you what I brought. I brought wisdom."

"Give it."

"Behold!"

And Colum, sitting upon the strewed fern that was his bed, rubbed his eyes that were heavy with weariness and fasting and long prayer. He could not see his Sleep now. It was gone as smoke that is licked up by the wind.

But on the ledge of the hole that was in the eastern wall of his cell he saw a bird. He leaned his elbow upon the leabhar-aifrionn that was by his side.[1] Then he spoke.

"Is there song upon thee, O Bru-dhearg?"

Then the Red-breast sang, and the singing was so sweet that tears came into the eyes of Colum, and he thought the sunlight that was streaming from the east was melted into that lilting sweet song. It was a hymn that the Bru-dhearg sang, and it was this:

Holy, Holy, Holy,

Christ upon the Cross:

My little nest was near,

Hidden in the moss.

Holy, Holy, Holy,

Christ was pale and wan:

His eyes beheld me singing

Bron, Bron, mo Bron![2]

Holy, Holy, Holy,

"Come near, O wee brown bird!"

Christ spake: and lo, I lighted

Upon the Living Word.

Holy, Holy, Holy,

I heard the mocking scorn!

But Holy, Holy, Holy

I sang against a thorn!

Holy, Holy, Holy,

Ah, his brow was bloody:

Holy, Holy, Holy,

All my breast was ruddy.

Holy, Holy, Holy,

Christ's-Bird shalt thou be:

Thus said Mary Virgin

There on Calvary.

Holy, Holy, Holy,

A wee brown bird am I:

But my breast is ruddy

For I saw Christ die.

Holy, Holy, Holy,

By this ruddy feather,

Colum, call thy monks, and

All the birds together.

And at that Colum rose. Awe was upon him, and joy.

He went out and told all to the monks. Then he said Mass out on the green sward. The yellow sunshine was warm upon his grey hair. The love of God was warm in his heart.

"Come, all ye birds!" he cried.

And lo, all the birds of the air flew nigh. The golden eagle soared from the Cuchullins in far-off Skye, and the osprey from the wild lochs of Mull; the gannet from above the clouds, and the fulmar and petrel from the green wave: the cormorant and the skua from the weedy rock, and the plover and the kestrel from the machar: the corbie and the raven from the moor, and the snipe and the bittern and the heron: the cuckoo and cushat from the woodland: the crane from the swamp, the lark from the sky, and the mavis and the merle from the green bushes: the yellowyite, the shilfa, and the lintie, the gyalvonn and the wren and the redbreast, one and all, every creature of the wings, they came at the bidding.

"Peace!" cried Colum.

"Peace!" cried all the Birds, and even the Eagle, the Kestrel, the Corbie, and the Raven cried Peace, Peace!

"I will say the Mass," said Colum the White.

And with that he said the Mass. And he blessed the birds.

When the last chant was sung, only the Bru-dhearg remained.

"Come, O Ruddy-Breast," said Colum, "and sing to us of the Christ."

Through a golden hour thereafter the Red-breast sang. Sweet was the joy of it.

At the end Colum said, "Peace! In the name of the Father, the Son, and the Holy Ghost."

Thereat Ardan the Pict bowed his head, and in a loud voice repeated—

"Sìth (shee)! An ainm an Athar, 's an mhic, 's an Spioraid Naoimh!"

And to this day the song of the Birds of Colum, as they are called in Hy, is Sìth—Sìth—Sìth—an—ainm—Chriosd——

"Peace—Peace—Peace—in the name of Christ!"

II

THE SABBATH OF THE FISHES AND THE FLIES

For three days Colum had fasted, save for a mouthful of meal at dawn, a piece of rye-bread at noon, and a mouthful of dulse and spring-water at sundown. On the night of the third day, Oran and Keir came to him in his cell. Colum was on his knees, lost in prayer. There was no sound there, save the faint whispered muttering of his lips, and on the plastered wall the weary buzzing of a fly.

"Master!" said Oran in a low voice, soft with pity and awe, "Master!"

But Colum took no notice. His lips still moved, and the tangled hairs below his nether lip shivered with his failing breath.

"Father!" said Keir, tender as a woman, "Father!"

Colum did not turn his eyes from the wall. The fly droned his drowsy hum upon the rough plaster. It crawled wearily for a space, then stopped. The slow hot drone filled the cell.

"Master," said Oran, "it is the will of the brethren that you break your fast. You are old, and God has your glory. Give us peace."

"Father," urged Keir, seeing that Colum kneeled unnoticingly, his lips still moving above his black beard, with the white hair of him falling about his head like a snowdrift slipping from a boulder. "Father, be pitiful! We hunger and thirst for your presence. We can fast no longer, yet have we no heart to break our fast if you are not with us. Come, holy one, and be of our company, and eat of the good broiled fish that awaiteth us. We perish for the benediction of thine eyes."

Then it was that Colum rose, and walked slowly towards the wall.

"Little black beast," he said to the fly that droned its drowsy hum and moved not at all; "little black beast, sure it is well I am knowing what you are. You are thinking you are going to get my blessing, you that have come out of hell for the soul of me!"

At that the fly flew heavily from the wall, and slowly circled round and round the head of Colum the White.

"What think you of that, brother Oran, brother Keir?" he asked in a low voice, hoarse because of his long fast and the weariness that was upon him.

"It is a fiend," said Oran.

"It is an angel," said Keir.

Thereupon the fly settled upon the wall again, and again droned his drowsy hot hum.

"Little black beast," said Colum, with the frown coming down into his eyes, "is it for peace you are here, or for sin? Answer, I conjure you in the name of the Father, the Son, and the Holy Ghost!"

"An ainm an Athar, 's an mhic, 's an Spioraid Naoimh," repeated Oran below his breath.

"An ainm an Athar, 's an mhic, 's an Spioraid Naoimh," repeated Keir below his breath.

Then the fly that was upon the wall flew up to the roof and circled to and fro. And it sang a beautiful song, and its song was this:

I

Praise be to God, and a blessing too at that, and a blessing!

For Colum the White, Colum the Dove, hath worshipped;

Yea, he hath worshipped and made of a desert a garden,

And out of the dung of men's souls hath made a sweet savour of burning.

II

A savour of burning, most sweet, a fire for the altar,

This he hath made in the desert; the hell-saved all gladden.

Sure he hath put his benison, too, on milch-cow and bullock,

On the fowls of the air, and the man-eyed seals, and the otter.

III

But where in his Dûn in the great blue mainland of Heaven

God the All-Father broodeth, where the harpers are harping
his glory;

There where He sitteth, where a river of ale poureth ever,

His great sword broken, His spear in the dust, He broodeth.

IV

And this is the thought that moves in his brain, as a cloud
filled with thunder

Moves through the vast hollow sky filled with the dust of
the stars:

What boots it the glory of Colum, since he maketh a
Sabbath to bless me,

And hath no thought of my sons in the deeps of the air and
the sea?

And with that the fly passed from their vision. In the cell
was a most wondrous sweet song, like the sound of far-off
pipes over water.

Oran said in a low voice of awe, "O our God!"

Keir whispered, white with fear, "O God, my God!"

But Colum rose, and took a scourge from where it hung on the wall. "It shall be for peace, Oran," he said, with a grim smile flitting like a bird above the nest of his black beard; "it shall be for peace, Keir!"

And with that he laid the scourge heavily upon the bent backs of Keir and Oran, nor stayed his hand, nor let his three days' fast weaken the deep piety that was in the might of his arm, and because of the glory to God.

Then, when he was weary, peace came into his heart, and he sighed "Amen!"

"Amen!" said Oran the monk.

"Amen!" said Keir the monk.

"And this thing hath been done," said Colum, "because of the evil wish of you and the brethren, that I should break my fast, and eat of fish, till God willeth it. And lo, I have learned a mystery. Ye shall all witness to it on the morrow, which is the Sabbath."

That night the monks wondered much. Only Oran and Keir cursed the fishes in the deeps of the sea and the flies in the deeps of the air.

On the morrow, when the sun was yellow on the brown sea-weed, and there was peace on the isle and upon the waters, Colum and the brotherhood went slowly towards the sea.

At the meadows that are close to the sea, the Saint stood still. All bowed their heads.

"O winged things of the air," cried Colum, "draw near!"

With that the air was full of the hum of innumerous flies, midges, bees, wasps, moths, and all winged insects. These settled upon the monks, who moved not, but praised God in silence. "Glory and praise to God," cried Colum, "behold the Sabbath of the children of God that inhabit the deeps of the air! Blessing and peace be upon them."

"Peace! Peace!" cried the monks, with one voice.

"In the name of the Father, the Son, and the Holy Ghost!" cried Colum the White, glad because of the glory to God.

"An ainm an Athar, 's an mhic, 's an Spioraid Naoimh," cried the monks, bowing reverently, and Oran and Keir deepest of all, because they saw the fly that was of Colum's cell leading the whole host, as though it were their captain, and singing to them a marvellous sweet song.

Oran and Keir testified to this thing, and all were full of awe and wonder, and Colum praised God.

Then the Saints and the brotherhood moved onward and went upon the rocks. When all stood ankle-deep in the sea-weed that was swaying in the tide, Colum cried:

"O finny creatures of the deep, draw near!"

And with that the whole sea shimmered as with silver and gold.

All the fishes of the sea, and the great eels, and the lobsters and the crabs, came in a swift and terrible procession. Great was the glory.

Then Colum cried, "O fishes of the Deep, who is your king?"

Whereupon the herring, the mackerel, and the dog-fish swam forward, and each claimed to be king. But the echo that ran from wave to wave said, The Herring is King.

Then Colum said to the mackerel: "Sing the song that is upon you!"

And the mackerel sang the song of the wild rovers of the sea, and the lust of pleasure.

Then Colum said, "But for God's mercy, I would curse you, O false fish."

Then he spake likewise to the dog-fish: and the dog-fish sang of slaughter and the chase, and the joy of blood.

And Colum said: "Hell shall be your portion."

And there was peace. And the Herring said:

"In the name of the Father, the Son, and the Holy Ghost!"

Whereat all that mighty multitude, ere they sank into the deep, waved their fins and their claws, each after his kind, and repeated as with one voice:

"An ainm an Athar, 's an mhic, 's an Spioraid Naoimh!"

And the glory that was upon the Sound of Iona was as though God trailed a starry net upon the waters, with a shining star in every little hollow, and a flowing moon of gold on every wave.

Then Colum the White put out both his arms, and blessed the children of God that are in the deeps of the sea and that are in the deeps of the air.

That is how Sabbath came upon all living things upon Hy that is called Iona, and within the air above Hy, and within the sea that is around Hy.

And the glory is Colum's.

III

THE MOON-CHILD

A year and a day before God bade Colum arise to the Feast
of Eternity, Pòl the Freckled, the youngest of the brethren,
came to him, on a night of the nights.

"The moon is among the stars, O Colum. By his own will,
and yours, old Murtagh that is this day with God, is to be
laid in the deep dry sand at the east end of the isle."

So the holy Saint rose from his bed of weariness, and went
and blessed the place that Murtagh lay in, and bade neither
the creeping worm nor any other creature to touch the
sacred dead. "Let God only," he said, "let God alone strip
that which he made to grow."
But on his way back sleep passed from him. The sweet salt
smell of the sea was in his nostrils: he heard the running of
a wave in all his blood.

At the cells he turned, and bade the brethren go in. "Peace
be with you," he sighed wearily.

Then he moved downwards towards the sea.

A great tenderness of late was upon Colum the Bishop.
Ever since he had blessed the fishes and the flies, the least
of the children of God, his soul had glowed in a whiter
flame. There were deep seas of compassion in his grey-blue
eyes. One night he had waked, because God was there.

"O Christ," he cried, bowing low his old grey head. "Sure,
ah sure, the gladness and the joy, because of the hour of the

hours."

But God said: "Not so, Colum, who keepest me upon the Cross. It is Murtagh, Murtagh the Druid that was, whose soul I am taking to the glory."

With that Colum rose in awe and great grief. There was no light in his cell. In the deep darkness, his spirit quailed. But lo, the beauty of his heart wrought a soft gleam about him, and in that moonshine of good deeds he rose and made his way to where Murtagh slept.

The old monk slept indeed. It was a sweet breath he drew—he, young and fair now, and laughing with peace under the apples in Paradise.

"O Murtagh," Colum cried, "and thee I thought the least of the brethren, because that thou wast a Druid, and loved not to see thy pagan kindred put to the sword if they would not repent. But, true, in my years I am becoming as a boy who learns, knowing nothing. God wash the sin of pride out of my life!"

At that a soft white shining, as of one winged and beautiful, stood beside the dead.

"Art thou Murtagh?" whispered Colum, in deep awe.

"No, I am not Murtagh," came as the breath of vanishing song.

"What art thou?"

"I am Peace," said the glory.

Thereupon Colum sank to his knees, sobbing with joy, for the sorrow that had been and was no more.

"Tell me, O White Peace," he murmured, "can Murtagh hearken, there under the apples where God is?"

"God's love is a wind that blows hitherward and hence. Speak, and thou shalt hear."

Colum spake. "O Murtagh my brother, tell me in what way it is that I still keep God crucified upon the Cross."

There was a sound in the cell as of the morning-laughter of children, of the singing of birds, of the sunlight streaming through the blue fields of Heaven.

Then Murtagh's voice came out of Paradise, sweet with the sweetness: honey-sweet it was, and clothed with deep awe because of the glory.

"Colum, servant of Christ, arise!"

Colum rose, and was as a leaf there, a leaf that is in the wind.

"Colum, thine hour is not yet come. I see it, bathing in the white light which is the Pool of Eternal Life, that is in the abyss where deep-rooted are the Gates of Heaven."

"And my sin, O Murtagh, my sin?"

"God is weary because thou hast not repented."

"O my God and my God! Sure, Murtagh, if that is so, it is so, but it is not for knowledge to me. Sure, O God, it is a blessing I have put on man and woman, on beast and bird and fish, on creeping things and flying things, on the green grass and the brown earth and the flowing wave, on the wind that cometh and goeth, and on the mystery of the flame! Sure, O God, I have sorrowed for all my sins: there is not one I have not fasted and prayed for. Sorrow upon me!—Is it accursed I am, or what is the evil that holdeth me by the hand?"

Then Murtagh, calling through sweet dreams and the rainbow-rain of happy tears that make that place so wondrous and so fair, spake once more:

"O Colum, blind art thou. Hast thou yet repented because after that thou didst capture the great black seal, that is a man under spells, thou, with thy monks, didst crucify him upon the great rock at the place where, long ago, thy coracle came ashore?"

"O Murtagh, favoured of God, will you not be explaining to Him that is King of the Elements, that this was because the seal who was called Black Angus wrought evil upon a mortal woman, and that of the sea-seed was sprung one who had no soul?"

But no answer came to that, and when Colum looked about him, behold there was no soft shining, but only the body of Murtagh the old monk. With a heavy heart, and his soul like a sinking boat in a sea of pain, he turned and went out into the night.

A fine, wonderful night it was. The moon lay low above the sea, and all the flowing gold and flashing silver of the rippling running water seemed to be a flood going that way and falling into the shining hollow splendour.

Through the sea-weed the old Saint moved, weary and sad. When he came to a sandy place he stopped. There, on a rock, he saw a little child. Naked she was, though clad with soft white moonlight. In her hair were brown weeds of the sea, gleaming golden because of the glow. In her hands was a great shell, and at that shell was her mouth. And she was singing this song; passing sweet to hear it was, with the sea-music that was in it:

A little lonely child am I

That have not any soul:

God made me but a homeless wave,

Without a goal.

A seal my father was, a seal

That once was man:

My mother loved him tho' he was

'Neath mortal ban.

He took a wave and drownèd her,

She took a wave and lifted him:

And I was born where shadows are

I' the sea-depths dim.

All through the sunny blue-sweet hours

I swim and glide in waters green;

Never by day the mournful shores

By me are seen.

But when the gloom is on the wave

A shell unto the shore I bring:

And then upon the rocks I sit

And plaintive sing.

O what is this wild song I sing,

With meanings strange and dim?

No soul am I, a wave am I,

And sing the Moon-Child's hymn.

Softly Colum drew nigh.

"Peace," he said. "Peace, little one. Ah tender little heart, peace!"

The child looked at him with wide sea-dusky eyes.

"Is it Colum the Holy you will be?"

"No, my fawn, my white dear babe: it is not Colum the Holy I am, but Colum the poor fool that knew not God!"

"Is it you, O Colum, that put the sorrow on my mother, who is the Sea-woman that lives in the whirlpool over there?"

"Ay, God forgive me!"

"Is it you, O Colum, that crucified the seal that was my father: him that was a man once, and that was called Black Angus?"

"Ay, God forgive me!"

"Is it you, O Colum, that bade the children of Hy run away from me, because I was a moon-child, and might win them by the sea-spell into the green wave?"

"Ay, God forgive me!"

"Sure, dear Colum, it was to the glory of God, it was?"

"Ay, He knoweth it, and can hear it, too, from Murtagh, who died this night."

"Look!"

And at that Colum looked, and in a moon-gold wave he saw Black Angus, the seal-man, drifting dark, and the eyes in his round head were the eyes of love. And beside the man-seal swam a woman fair to see, and she looked at him with joy, and with joy at the Moon-Child that was her own, and at Colum with joy.

Thereupon Colum fell upon his knees and cried—

"Give me thy sorrow, wild woman of the sea!"

"Peace to you, Colum," she answered, and sank into the shadow-thridden wave.

"Give my thy death and crucifixion, O Angus-dhu!" cried the Saint, shaking with the sorrow.

"Peace to you, Colum," answered the man-seal, and sank into the dusky quietudes of the deep.

"Ah, bitter heart o' me! Teach me the way to God, O little child," cried Colum the old, turning to where the Moon-Child was!

But lo, the glory and the wonder!

It was a little naked child that looked at him with healing eyes, but there were no sea-weeds in her hair, and no shell in the little wee hands of her. For now, it was a male Child that was there, shining with a light from within: and in his fair sunny hair was a shadowy crown of thorns, and in his hand was a pearl of great price.

"O Christ, my God," said Colum, with failing voice.

"It is thine now, O Colum," said the Moon-Child, holding out to him the shining pearl of great price.

"What is it, O Lord my God?" whispered the old servant of God that was now glad with the gladness: "what is this, thy boon?"

"Perfect Peace."

And that is all.

(To God be the Glory. Amen.)

THE MELANCHOLY OF ULAD

In the sea-loch now known as that of Tarbert of Loch Fyne, but in the old far-off days named the Haven of the Foray, there was once a grianân, a sunbower, of so great a beauty that thereto the strings of the singing men's clarsachs vibrated even in far-away Ireland.

This was in the days before the yellow-haired men out of Lochlin came swarming in their galleys, along the lochs and fjords of the west. So long ago was it that none knows if Ulad sang his song to Fand before Diarmid the Fair was slain on the narrow place between the two lochs, or if it were when Colum's white-robes were wont to come out of the open sea up the Loch of the Swans, that is now West Loch Tarbert, so as to reach the inlands.

But of what import is the whitherset of bygone days, where the tale of the years and of the generations is as that of autumn's leaves?

Ulad was there, the poet-king: and Fand, whom he loved: and Life and Death.

Ian Mòr, of whom I have written, told me the tale many years ago. I cannot recall all he said, and I know well that the echo of ancient music that was below his words, as he spoke in the gloaming before the peats, and in the ancient tongue of our people, is not now what it was then.

None knows whence Ulad came. In the Isles of the West men said he was a prince out of the realm of the Ultonians; but there, in the north of Eiré, they said he was a king in the southlands. Art the White, the wise old Ardrigh of the peoples who dwelt among the lake-lands far south, spoke of Ulad as one born under a solitary star on the night of the Festival of Beltane, and told that he came out of an ancient land north or south of Muirnict, the sea which has the feet of Wales and Cornwall upon its sunrise side and the rocks and sands of Armorica upon that where the light reddens the west. But upon Ioua, that is now Iona, there was one wiser even than Art the White, Dùach the Druid: and when questioned as to Ulad the poet-king, he said he was of the ancient people that dwelt among the inlands of Alba, the old race that had known the divine folk, the Tuatha-de-Danann, when they were seen of men and no mortality was upon their sweet clay. The islanders were awed by what Dùach told them, for what manner of man could this be who had seen Merlin going tranced through the woods, playing upon a reed, with wolves fawning upon him, and the noise of eagles' wings ruffling the greenglooms of the forest overhead?

And of Fand, who knows aught? Bêl the Harper, whose songs and playing made women's hearts melt like wax, and in men wrought either intolerable longing or put sudden swift flames into the blood, sang of her. And what he sang was this: that Ulad had fared once to Hy Bràsil and had there beheld a garth of white blooms, fragrant and wonderful, under the hither base of a rainbow. These flowers he had gathered, and warmed all night against his breast, and at dawn breathed into them. When the sunbreak slid a rising line along the dawn he blew a frith across the palm of his left hand. What had been white blooms, made rosy with his breath and warm against his side, was a woman. It was Fand.

Who, then, can tell whether Ulad were old or young when he came to the Haven of the Foray. He had the old ancient wisdom, and mayhap knew how to wrap himself round with the green life that endures.

None knew of his being in that place, till, one set of a disastrous day, a birlinn drove in before the tempest sweeping from the isle of Arran up the great sea-loch of Fionn. The oarsmen drew breath when the headlands were past, and then stared with amaze. Overagainst the bay in the little rocky promontory on the north side was a house built wondrously, and that where no house had stood, and after a fashion that not one of them had seen, and all marvelled with wide eyes. The sunset flamed upon it, so that its shining walls were glorious. A small round grianân it was, but built all of blocks and stones of hill-crystal, and upborne upon four great pine-boles driven deep into the tangled grass and sand, with these hung about with deerskins and fells of wolf and other savagery.

Before this grianân the men in the birlinn, upon whom silence had fallen, and whose listless oars made no lapping upon the foam-white small leaping waves of the haven, beheld a man lying face downward.

For a time they thought the man was dead. It was one, they said, some great one, who had perished at the feet of his desire. Others thought he was a king who had come there to die alone, as Conn the Solitary had done, when he had known all that man can know. And some feared that the prone man was a demon, and the shining grianân a dreadful place of spells. The howling of a wolf, in the opposite glen that is called Strathnamara, brought sweat upon their backs: for when the half-human wish evil upon men they hide their faces, and the howling of a she-wolf is heard.

But of a sudden the helmsman made a sign. "It is Ulad," he whispered hoarsely, because of the salt in his throat after that day of flight and long weariness: "It is Ulad the Wonder-Smith."

Then all there were glad, for each man knew that Ulad the Wonder-Smith, that was a poet and a king, wrought no ill against any clan, and that wherever he was the swords slept.

Nevertheless they marvelled much that he was there alone, and in that silence, with his face prone upon the wilderness, while the sunset flamed overagainst the grianân that was now like wine, or like springing blood light and wonderful. But as tide and wind brought the birlinn close upon the shore, they heard a twofold noise, a rumour of strange sound. One looked at the other, with amaze that grew into fear. For the twofold sound was wrought of the muffled sobs and prayers of the man that lay upon the grass and of the laughter of the woman that was unseen, but who was within the grianân.

Connla, the helmsman and leader of the seafarers, waved to his fellows to pull the birlinn close in among the weedy masses which hung from the rocks. When the galley lay there, all but hidden, and each man's head was beneath the wrack, Connla rose. Slowly he moved to where Ulad lay, face downward, upon the silt of sand and broken rock that was in front of the grianân. But, before he could speak, the young king rose, though not seeing the newcomer, and, looking upon the sunbower, whence the laughter suddenly ceased, raised his arms.

Then, when he had raised his arms, song was upon his lips. It was a strange chant that Connla heard, and had the sound in it of the wind far out at sea, or of a tempest moving across treeless moors, mournful, wild, filled with ancient sorrow and a crying that none can interpret. And the words of it, familiar to the helmsman, and yet with a strange lip-life upon them, were as these:—

Ah you in the grianân there, whose laughter is on me as fire-flames,

What of the sorrow of sorrows that is mine because of my loving—

You that came to me out of the place where the rainbows are builded,

Is it woman you are, O Fand, who laughest up there in thy silence?

Sure, I have loved thee through storm and peace, through the day and the night;

Sure, I have set the singing of songs to a marvellous swan-song for thee,

And death I have dared, and life have I dared, and gloom and the grave,

And yet, O Fand, thou laughest down on my pain, on my pain, O Fand.

All things have I thrown away gladly only to win thee—

Kingship and lordship of men, the fame of the sword, and all good things—

For in thee at the last, I dreamed, in thee, O Fand, Queen of Women,

I had found all that a man may find, and was as the gods who die not.

But what of all this to me, who am Ulad the King, the Harper,

Ulad the Singer of Songs that are fire in the hearts of the hearers,

Ulad the Wonder-Smith, who can bridle the winds and the billows,

Can lay waste the greatest of Dûns or build grianâns here in the wilds—

What of all this to me, who am only a man that seeketh,

That seeketh for ever and ever the Soul that is fellow to his—

The Soul that is thee, O Fand, who wert born of flowers 'neath the rainbow,

Breathed with my breath, warmed at my breast, O Fand, whom I love and I worship?

For all things are vain unto me, but one thing only, and that not vain is—

My Dream, my Passion, my Hope, my Fand, whom I won from Hy Bràsil:

O Dream of my life, my Glory, O Rose of the World, my Dream,

Lo, death for Ulad the King, if thou failest, for all that I am of the Danann who die not.

And when he had chanted these words, Ulad, who was young and wondrous fair to look upon, held out his arms to Fand, whom yet he did not see, for she was within the grianân.

"Then, if even not yet at the setting of the day," the king muttered, "patience shall be upon me till the coming of a new day, and then it may be that Fand will hear my prayer."

And so the night fell. But when the screaming of the gulls came over the loch, and the plaintive crying of the lapwings was upon the moorland, and the smell of loneroid and bracken was heavy in the wind-fallen stillness, Ulad turned, for he felt a touch upon his shoulder.

It was Connla who touched him, and he knew the man. He had the old wisdom of knowing all that is in the mind by looking into the eyes, and he knew how the man had come there.

"Let the men who are your men, O Connla, move away from here in their birlinn, and go farther up into the haven."

And because he was a Wonder-Smith, and knew all, the islander did as Ulad bade, and without question. But when they were alone again he spoke.

"Ulad, great lord, I am a man who is as idle sand beneath the feet of you who know the ancient wisdom, and are young with imperishing years, and are a great king in some land I know not of—so, at the least, men say. But I know one thing that you do not know."

"If you will tell me one thing that I do not know, O Connla, you shall have your heart's desire."

Connla laughed at that.

"Not even you, O Ulad, can give me my heart's desire."

"And what will that desire be then, you whom the islesmen call Connla the Wise?"

"That one might see in the dew the footsteps of old years returning."

"That thing, Connla, I cannot do."

"And yet thou wouldst do what is a thing as vain as that?"

"Speak. I will listen."

Then Connla drew close to Ulad, and whispered in his ear. Thereafter he gave him a hollow reed with holes in it, such as the shepherding folk use on the hills. And with that he went away into the darkness.

When the moon rose, Ulad took the reed and played upon it. While he played, scales fell from his eyes, and dreams passed from his brain, and his heart grew light. Then he sang:

Come forth, Fand, come forth, beautiful Fand, my woman, my fawn,

The smell of thy falling hair is sweet as the breath of the wild-brier—

I weary of this white moonshine who love better the white discs of thy breasts,

And the secret song of the gods is faint beside the craving in my blood.

Fand, Fand, Fand, white one, who art no dream but a woman,

Come forth from the grianân, or lo by the word of me, Ulad the King,

Forth shalt thou come as a she-wolf, and no more be a woman,

Come forth to me, Fand, who am now as a flame for thy burning!

Thereupon a low laugh was heard, and Fand came forth out of the grianân. White and beautiful she was, the fairest of all women, and Ulad was glad. When near, she whispered in his ears, and hand-in-hand they went back into the grianân.

At dawn Ulad looked upon the beauty of Fand, and he saw she was as a flower.

"O fair and beautiful Dream," he whispered—but of a sudden Fand laughed in her sleep, and he remembered what

Connla the Wise had told him.

"Woman," Ulad muttered then, "I see well that thou art not my Dream, but only a woman." And with that he half-rose from her.

Fand opened her eyes, and the beauty of them was greater for the light that was there.

"Then thou art only Ulad, a man?" she cried, and she put her arms about him, and kissed him on the lips and on the breast, sobbing low as with a strange gladness—"I will follow thee, Ulad, to death, for I am thy woman."

"Ay," he said, looking beyond her, "if I feed thee, and call thee my woman, and find pleasure in thee, and give thee my manhood."

"And what else wouldst thou, O Ulad?" Fand asked, wondering.

"I am Ulad the Lonely," he answered: this, and no more.

Then, later, he took the hollow reed again, and again played.

And when he had played he looked at Fand. He saw into her heart, and into her brain.

"I have dreamed my dream," he said; "but I am still Ulad the Wonder-Smith."

With that he blew a frith across the palm of his left hand, and said this thing:—

"O woman that would not come to me, when I called out of that within me which is I myself, farewell!"

And with that Fand was a drift of white flowers there upon the deerskins.

Then once more Ulad spoke.

"O woman, that heeded no bitter prayer which I made, but at the last came only as a she-wolf to the wolf, farewell!"

And with that a wind-eddy scattered the white flowers upon the deerskins, and they wavered hither and thither, and some were stained by the pale wandering fires of a rainbow that drifted over that place, then as now the haunt of these cloudy splendours, forever woven there out of sun and mist.

At noon, the seafarers came towards the grianân with songs, and offerings.

But Ulad was not there.

ULA AND URLA

"Rose of all Roses, Rose of all the World!

You, too, have come where the dim tides are hurled

Upon the wharves of sorrow, and heard ring

The bell that calls us on: the sweet far thing.

Beauty grown sad with its eternity

Made you of us, and of the dim grey sea."

Ula and Urla were under vow to meet by the Stone of Sorrow. But Ula, dying first, stumbled blindfold when he passed the Shadowy Gate; and, till Urla's hour was upon her, she remembered not.[3]

These were the names that had been given to them in the north isles, when the birlinn that ran down the war-galley of the vikings brought them before the Maormor.

No word had they spoken that day, and no name. They were of the Gael, though Ula's hair was yellow, and though his eyes were blue as the heart of a wave. They would ask nothing, for both were in love with death. The Maormor of Siol Tormaid looked at Urla, and his desire gnawed at his heart. But he knew what was in her mind, because he saw into it through her eyes, and he feared the sudden slaying in the dark.

Nevertheless, he brooded night and day upon her beauty. Her skin was more white than the foam of the moon: her eyes were as a star-lit dewy dusk. When she moved, he saw her like a doe in the fern: when she stooped, it was as the fall of wind-swayed water. In his eyes there was a shimmer as of the sunflood in a calm sea. In that dazzle he was led astray.

"Go," he said to Ula, on a day of the days. "Go: the men of Siol Torquil will take you to the south isles, and so you can hale to your own place, be it Eirèann or Manannan, or wherever the south wind puts its hand upon your home."

It was on that day Ula spoke for the first time.

"I will go, Coll mac Torcall; but I go not alone. Urla that I love goes whither I go."

"She is my spoil. But, man out of Eirèann—for so I know you to be, because of the manner of your speech—tell me this: Of what clan and what place are you, and whence is Urla come; and by what shore was it that the men of Lochlin whom we slew took you and her out of the sea, as you swam against the sun, with waving swords upon the strand when the viking-boat carried you away?"

"How know you these things?" asked Ula, that had been Isla, son of the king of Islay.

"One of the sea-rovers spake before he died."

"Then let the viking speak again. I have nought to say."

With that the Maormor frowned, but said no more. That eve Ula was seized, as he walked in the dusk by the sea, singing low to himself an ancient song.

"Is it death?" he said, remembering another day when he and Eilidh, that they called Urla, had the same asking upon their lips.

"It is death."

Ula frowned, but spake no word for a time. Then he spake.

"Let me say one word with Urla."

"No word canst thou have. She, too, must die."

Ula laughed low at that.

"I am ready," he said. And they slew him with a spear.

When they told Urla, she rose from the deerskins and went down to the shore. She said no word then. But she stooped, and she put her lips upon his cold lips, and she whispered in his unhearing ear.

That night Coll mac Torcall went secretly to where Urla was. When he entered, a groan came to his lips and there was froth there: and that was because the spear that had slain Ula was thrust betwixt his shoulders by one who stood in the shadow. He lay there till the dawn. When they found Coll the Maormor he was like a seal speared upon a rock, for he had his hands out, and his head was between them, and his face was downward.

"Eat dust, slain wolf," was all that Eilidh, whom they called Urla, said, ere she moved away from that place in the darkness of the night.

When the sun rose, Urla was in a glen among the hills. A man who shepherded there took her to his mate. They gave her milk, and because of her beauty and the frozen silence of her eyes, bade her stay with them and be at peace.

They knew in time that she wished death. But first, there was the birthing of the child.

"It was Isla's will," she said to the woman. Ula was but the shadow of a bird's wing: an idle name. And she, too, was Eilidh once more.

"It was death he gave you when he gave you the child," said the woman once.

"It was life," answered Eilidh, with her eyes filled with the shadow of dream. And yet another day the woman said to her that it would be well to bear the child and let it die: for beauty was like sunlight on a day of clouds, and if she were to go forth young and alone and so wondrous fair, she would have love, and love is best.

"Truly, love is best," Eilidh answered. "And because Isla loved me, I would that another Isla came into the world and sang his songs—the songs that were so sweet, and the songs that he never sang, because I gave him death when I gave him life. But now he shall live again, and he and I shall be in one body, in him that I carry now."

At that the woman understood, and said no more. And so the days grew out of the nights, and the dust of the feet of one month was in the eyes of that which followed after; and this until Eilidh's time was come.

Dusk after dusk, Ula that was Isla the Singer, waited by the Stone of Sorrow. Then a great weariness came upon him. He made a song there, where he lay in the narrow place; the last song that he made, for after that he heard no trampling of the hours.

The swift years slip and slide adown the steep;

The slow years pass; neither will come again.

Yon huddled years have weary eyes that weep,

These laugh, these moan, these silent frown, these plain,

These have their lips acurl with proud disdain.

O years with tears, and tears through weary years,

How weary I who in your arms have lain:

Now, I am tired: the sound of slipping spears

Moves soft, and tears fall in a bloody rain,

And the chill footless years go over me who am slain.

I hear, as in a wood, dim with old light, the rain,

Slow falling; old, old, weary, human tears:

And in the deepening dark my comfort is my Pain,

Sole comfort left of all my hopes and fears,

Pain that alone survives, gaunt hound of the shadowy years.

But, at the last, after many days, he stirred. There was a song in his ears.

He listened. It was like soft rain in a wood in June. It was like the wind laughing among the leaves.

Then his heart leaped. Sure, it was the voice of Eilidh!

"Eilidh! Eilidh! Eilidh!" he cried. But a great weariness came upon him again. He fell asleep, knowing not the little hand that was in his, and the small, flower-sweet body that was warm against his side.

Then the child that was his looked into the singer's heart, and saw there a mist of rainbows, and midway in that mist was the face of Eilidh, his mother.

Thereafter, the little one looked into his brain that was so still, and he saw the music that was there: and it was the voice of Eilidh his mother.

And, again, the birdeen, that had the blue of Isla's eyes and the dream of Eilidh's, looked into Ula's sleeping soul: and he saw that it was not Isla nor yet Eilidh, but that it was like unto himself, who was made of Eilidh and Isla.

For a long time the child dreamed. Then he put his ear to Isla's brow, and listened. Ah, the sweet songs that he heard. Ah, bitter-sweet moonseed of song! Into his life they passed, echo after echo, strain after strain, wild air after wild sweet air.

"Isla shall never die," whispered the child, "for Eilidh loved him. And I am Isla and Eilidh."

Then the little one put his hands above Isla's heart. There was a flame there, that the Grave quenched not.

"O flame of love!" sighed the child, and he clasped it to his breast: and it was a moonshine glory about the two hearts that he had, the heart of Isla and the heart of Eilidh, that were thenceforth one.

At dawn he was no longer there. Already the sunrise was warm upon him where he lay, new-born, upon the breast of Eilidh.

"It is the end," murmured Isla when he waked. "She has never come. For sure, now, the darkness and the silence."

Then he remembered the words of Maol the Druid, he that was a seer, and had told him of Orchil, the dim goddess who is under the brown earth, in a vast cavern, where she weaves at two looms. With one hand she weaves life upward through the grass; with the other she weaves death downward through the mould; and the sound of the weaving is Eternity, and the name of it in the green world is Time. And, through all, Orchil weaves the weft of Eternal Beauty, that passeth not, though its soul is Change.

And these were the words of Orchil, on the lips of Maol the Druid, that was old, and knew the mystery of the Grave.

When thou journeyest towards the Shadowy Gate take neither Fear with thee nor Hope, for both are abashed hounds of silence in that place; but take only the purple nightshade for sleep, and a vial of tears and wine, tears that shall be known unto thee and old wine of love. So shalt thou have thy silent festival, ere the end.

So therewith Isla, having, in his weariness, the nightshade of sleep, and in his mind the slow dripping rain of familiar tears, and deep in his heart the old wine of love, bowed his head.

It was well to have lived, since life was Eilidh. It was well to cease to live, since Eilidh came no more.

Then suddenly he raised his head. There was music in the green world above. A sunray opened the earth about him: staring upward he beheld Angus Ogue.

"Ah, fair face of the god of youth," he sighed. Then he saw the white birds that fly about the head of Angus Ogue, and he heard the music that his breath made upon the harp of the wind.

"Arise," said Angus; and, when he smiled the white birds flashed their wings and made a mist of rainbows.

"Arise," said Angus Ogue again, and, when he spoke, the spires of the grass quivered to a wild, sweet haunting air.

So Isla arose, and the sun shone upon him, and his shadow passed into the earth. Orchil wove it into her web of death.

"Why dost thou wait here by the Stone of Sorrow, Isla that was called Ula at the end?"

"I wait for Eilidh, who cometh not."

At that the wind-listening god stooped and laid his head upon the grass.

"I hear the coming of a woman's feet," he said, and he rose.

"Eilidh! Eilidh!" cried Isla, and the sorrow of his cry was a moan in the web of Orchil.

Angus Ogue took a branch, and put the cool greenness against his cheek.

"I hear the beating of a heart," he said.

"Eilidh! Eilidh! Eilidh!" Isla cried, and the tears that were in his voice were turned by Angus into dim dews of remembrance in the babe-brain that was the brain of Isla and Eilidh.

"I hear a word," said Angus Ogue, "and that word is a flame of joy."

Isla listened. He heard a singing of birds. Then, suddenly, a glory came into the shine of the sun.

"I have come, Isla my king!"

It was the voice of Eilidh. He bowed his head, and swayed; for it was his own life that came to him.

"Eilidh!" he whispered.

And so, at the last, Isla came into his kingdom.

But are they gone, these twain, who loved with deathless love? Or is this a dream that I have dreamed?

Afar in an island-sanctuary that I shall not see again, where the wind chants the blind oblivious rune of Time, I have heard the grasses whisper: Time never was, Time is not.

THE DARK NAMELESS ONE

One day this summer I sailed with Padruic Macrae and Ivor McLean, boatmen of Iona, along the south-western reach of the Ross of Mull.

The whole coast of the Ross is indescribably wild and desolate. From Feenafort (Fhionnphort), opposite Balliemore of Icolmkill, to the hamlet of Earraid Lighthouse, it were hardly exaggeration to say that the whole tract is uninhabited by man and unenlivened by any green thing. It is the haunt of the cormorant and the seal.

No one who has not visited this region can realise its barrenness. Its one beauty is the faint bloom which lies upon it in the sunlight—a bloom which becomes as the glow of an inner flame when the sun westers without cloud or mist. This is from the ruddy hue of the granite, of which all that wilderness is wrought.

It is a land tortured by the sea, scourged by the sea-wind. A myriad lochs, fiords, inlets, passages, serrate its broken frontiers. Innumerable islets and reefs, fanged like ravenous wolves, sentinel every shallow, lurk in every strait. He must be a skilled boatman who would take the Sound of Earraid and penetrate the reaches of the Ross.

There are many days in the months of peace, as the islanders call the period from Easter till the autumnal equinox, when Earraid and the rest of Ross seem under a spell. It is the spell of beauty. Then the yellow light of the sun is upon the tumbled masses and precipitous shelves and ledges, ruddy petals or leaves of that vast Flower of Granite. Across it the cloud shadows trail their purple elongations, their scythe-sweep curves, and abrupt evanishing floodings of warm dusk. From wet boulder to boulder, from crag to shelly crag, from fissure to fissure, the sea ceaselessly weaves a girdle of foam. When the wide luminous stretch of waters beyond—green near the land, and farther out all of a living blue, interspersed with wide alleys of amethyst—is white with the sea-horses, there is such a laughter of surge and splash all the way from Slugan-dubh to the Rudha-nam-Maol-Mòra, or to the tide-swept promontory of the Sgeireig-a'-Bhochdaidh, that, looking inland, one sees through a rainbow-shimmering veil of ever-flying spray.

But the sun spell is even more fugitive upon the face of this wild land than the spell of beauty upon a woman. So runs one of our proverbs: as the falling of the wave, as the fading of the leaf, so is the beauty of a woman, unless—ah, that unless, and the indiscoverable fount of joy that can only be come upon by hazard once in life, and thereafter only in dreams, and the Land of the Rainbow that is never reached, and the green sea-doors of Tir-na-thonn, that open now no more to any wandering wave!

It was from Ivor McLean, on that day, I heard the strange tale of his kinsman Murdoch, the tale of "The Ninth Wave" that I have told elsewhere. It was Padruic, however, who told me of the Sea-witch of Earraid.

"Yes," he said, "I have heard of the each-uisge (the sea-beast, sea-kelpie, or water-horse), but I have never seen it with the eyes. My father and my brother knew of it. But this thing I know, and this what we call an-cailleach-uisge (the siren or water-witch); the cailliach, mind you, not the maighdeann-mhàra (the mermaid), who means no harm. May she hear my saying it! The cailliach is old and clad in weeds, but her voice is young, and she always sits so that the light is in the eyes of the beholder. She seems to him young also, and fair. She has two familiars in the form of seals, one black as the grave, and the other white as the shroud that is in the grave; and these sometimes upset a boat, if the sailor laughs at the uisge-cailliach's song.

"A man netted one of those seals, more than a hundred years ago, with his herring-trawl, and dragged it into the boat; but the other seal tore at the net so savagely, with its head and paws over the bows, that it was clear no net would long avail. The man heard them crying and screaming, and then talking low and muttering, like women in a frenzy. In his fear he cast the nets adrift, all but a small portion that was caught in the thwarts. Afterwards, in this portion, he found a tress of woman's hair. And that is just so: to the Stones be it said.

"The grandson of this man, Tòmais McNair, is still living, a shepherd on Eilean-Uamhain, beyond Lunga in the Cairnburg Isles. A few years ago, off Callachan Point, he saw the two seals, and heard, though he did not see, the cailliach. And that which I tell you—Christ's Cross before me—is a true thing."

All the time that Phadruic was speaking, I saw that Ivor McLean looked away: either as though he heard nothing, or did not wish to hear. There was dream in his eyes; I saw that, so said nothing for a time.

"What is it, Ivor?" I asked at last, in a low voice. He started, and looked at me strangely.

"What will you be asking that for? What are you doing in my mind, that is secret?"

"I see that you are brooding over something. Will you not tell me?"

"Tell her," said Phadruic quietly.

But Ivor kept silent. There was a look in his eyes which I understood. Thereafter we sailed on, with no word in the boat at all.

That night, a dark, rainy night it was, with an uplift wind beating high over against the hidden moon, I went to the cottage where Ivor McLean lived with his old deaf mother, deaf nigh upon twenty years, ever since the night of the nights when she heard the women whisper that Callum, her husband, was among the drowned, after a death-wind had blown.

When I entered, he was sitting before the flaming coal-fire; for on Iona now, by decree of MacCailin Mòr, there is no more peat burned.

"You will tell me now, Ivor?" was all I said.

"Yes; I will be telling you now. And the reason why I did not tell you before was because it is not a wise or a good thing to tell ancient stories about the sea while still on the running wave. Macrae should not have done that thing. It may be we shall suffer for it when next we go out with the nets. We were to go to-night; but no, not I, no no, for sure, not for all the herring in the Sound."

"Is it an ancient sgeul, Ivor?"

"Ay. I am not for knowing the age of these things. It may be as old as the days of the Féinn for all I know. It has come down to us. Alasdair MacAlasdair of Tiree, him that used to boast of having all the stories of Colum and Brighde, it was he told it to the mother of my mother, and she to me."

"What is it called?"

"Well, this and that; but there is no harm in saying it is called the Dark Nameless One."

"The Dark Nameless One!"

"It is this way. But will you ever have been hearing of the MacOdrums of Uist?"

"Ay: the Sliochd-nan-ròn."

"That is so. God knows. The Sliochd-nan-ròn ... the progeny of the Seal.... Well, well, no man knows what moves in the shadow of life. And now I will be telling you that old ancient tale, as it was given to me by the mother of my mother."

On a day of the days, Colum was walking alone by the sea-shore. The monks were at the hoe or the spade, and some milking the kye, and some at the fishing. They say it was on the first day of the Faoilleach Geamhraidh, the day that is called Am fheill Brighde.

The holy man had wandered on to where the rocks are, opposite to Soa. He was praying and praying, and it is said that whenever he prayed aloud, the barren egg in the nest would quicken, and the blighted bud unfold, and the butterfly cleave its shroud.

Of a sudden he came upon a great black seal, lying silent on the rocks, with wicked eyes.

"My blessing upon you, O Ròn," he said with the good kind courteousness that was his.

"Droch spadadh ort," answered the seal. "A bad end to you, Colum of the Gown."

"Sure, now," said Colum angrily, "I am knowing by that curse that you are no friend of Christ, but of the evil pagan faith out of the north. For here I am known ever as Colum the White, or as Colum the Saint; and it is only the Picts and the wanton Normen who deride me because of the holy white robe I wear."

"Well, well," replied the seal, speaking the good Gaelic as though it were the tongue of the deep sea, as God knows it may be for all you, I, or the blind wind can say; "Well, well, let that thing be: it's a wave-way here or a wave-way there. But now if it is a Druid you are, whether of Fire or of Christ, be telling me where my woman is, and where my little daughter."

At this, Colum looked at him for a long while. Then he knew.

"It is a man you were once, O Ròn?"

"Maybe ay and maybe no."

"And with that thick Gaelic that you have, it will be out of the north isles you come?"

"That is a true thing."

"Now I am for knowing at last who and what you are. You are one of the race of Odrum the Pagan."

"Well, I am not denying it, Colum. And what is more, I am Angus MacOdrum, Aonghas mac Torcall mhic Odrum, and the name I am known by is Black Angus."

"A fitting name too," said Colum the Holy, "because of the black sin in your heart, and the black end God has in store for you."

At that Black Angus laughed.

"Why is there laughter upon you, Man-Seal?"

"Well, it is because of the good company I'll be having. But, now, give me the word: Are you for having seen or heard aught of a woman called Kirsteen McVurich?"

"Kirsteen—Kirsteen—that is the good name of a nun it is, and no sea-wanton!"

"Oh, a name here or a name there is soft sand. And so you cannot be for telling me where my woman is?"

"No."

"Then a stake for your belly, and the nails through your hands, thirst on your tongue, and the corbies at your eyne!"

And, with that, Black Angus louped into the green water, and the hoarse wild laugh of him sprang into the air and fell dead against the cliff like a wind-spent mew.

Colum went slowly back to the brethren, brooding deep. "God is good," he said in a low voice, again and again; and each time that he spoke there came a fair sweet daisy into the grass, or a yellow bird rose up, with song to it for the first time wonderful and sweet to hear.

As he drew near to the House of God he met Murtagh, an old monk of the ancient old race of the isles.

"Who is Kirsteen McVurich, Murtagh?" he asked.

"She was a good servant of Christ, she was, in the south isles, O Colum, till Black Angus won her to the sea."

"And when was that?"

"Nigh upon a thousand years ago."

At that Colum stared in amaze. But Murtagh was a man of truth, nor did he speak in allegories. "Ay, Colum, my father, nigh upon a thousand years ago."

"But can mortal sin live as long as that?"

"Ay, it endureth. Long, long ago, before Oisìn sang, before Fionn, before Cuchullin was a glorious great prince, and in the days when the Tuatha-De Danànn were sole lords in all green Banba, Black Angus made the woman Kirsteen McVurich leave the place of prayer and go down to the sea-shore, and there he leaped upon her and made her his prey, and she followed him into the sea."

"And is death above her now?"

"No. She is the woman that weaves the sea-spells at the wild place out yonder that is known as Earraid: she that is called an-cailleach-uisge, the sea-witch."

"Then why was Black Angus for the seeking her here and the seeking her there?"

"It is the Doom. It is Adam's first wife she is, that sea-witch over there, where the foam is ever in the sharp fangs of the rocks."

"And who will he be?"

"His body is the body of Angus the son of Torcall of the race of Odrum, for all that a seal he is to the seeming; but the soul of him is Judas."

"Black Judas, Murtagh?"

"Ay, Black Judas, Colum."

But with that, Ivor Macrae rose abruptly from before the fire, saying that he would speak no more that night. And truly enough there was a wild, lone, desolate cry in the wind, and a slapping of the waves one upon the other with an eerie laughing sound, and the screaming of a sea-mew that was like a human thing.

So I touched the shawl of his mother, who looked up with startled eyes and said, "God be with us"; and then I opened the door, and the salt smell of the wrack was in my nostrils, and the great drowning blackness of the night.

THE SMOOTHING OF THE HAND

Glad am I that wherever and whenever I listen intently I can hear the looms of Nature weaving Beauty and Music. But some of the most beautiful things are learned otherwise—by hazard, in the Way of Pain, or at the Gate of Sorrow.

I learned two things on the day when I saw Sheumas McIan dead upon the heather. He of whom I speak was the son of Ian McIan Alltnalee, but was known throughout the home straths and the countries beyond as Sheumas Dhu, Black James, or, to render the subtler meaning implied in this instance, James the Dark One. I had wondered occasionally at the designation, because Sheumas, if not exactly fair, was not dark. But the name was given to him, as I learned later, because, as commonly rumoured, he knew that which he should not have known.

I had been spending some weeks with Alasdair McIan and his wife Silis (who was my foster-sister), at their farm of Ardoch, high in a remote hill country. One night we were sitting before the peats, listening to the wind crying amid the corries, though, ominously as it seemed to us, there was not a breath in the rowan-tree that grew in the sun's-way by the house. Silis had been singing, but silence had come upon us. In the warm glow from the fire we saw each other's faces. There the silence lay, strangely still and beautiful, as snow in moonlight. Silis's song was one of the Dana Spioradail, known in Gaelic as the Hymn of the Looms. I cannot recall it, nor have I ever heard or in any way encountered it again.

It had a lovely refrain, I know not whether its own or added by Silis. I have heard her chant it to other runes and songs. Now, when too late, my regret is deep that I did not take from her lips more of those sorrowful, strange songs or chants, with their ancient Celtic melodies, so full of haunting sweet melancholy, which she loved so well. It was with this refrain that, after a long stillness, she startled us that October night. I remember the sudden light in the eyes of Alasdair McIan, and the beat at my heart, when, like rain in a wood, her voice fell unawares upon us out of the silence:

Oh! oh! ohrone, arone! Oh! oh! mo ghraidh, mo chridhe! Oh! oh! mo ghraidh, mo chridhe![4]

The wail, and the sudden break in the second line, had always upon me an effect of inexpressible pathos. Often that sad wind-song has been in my ears, when I have been thinking of many things that are passed and are passing.

I know not what made Silis so abruptly begin to sing, and with that wailing couplet only, or why she lapsed at once into silence again. Indeed, my remembrance of the incident at all is due to the circumstance that shortly after Silis had turned her face to the peats again, a knock came to the door, and then Sheumas Dhu entered.

"Why do you sing that lament, Silis, sister of my father?" he asked, after he had seated himself beside me, and spread his thin hands against the peat glow, so that the flame seemed to enter within the flesh.

Silis turned to her nephew, and looked at him, as I thought, questioningly. But she did not speak. He, too, said nothing more, either forgetful of his question, or content with what he had learned or failed to learn through her silence.

The wind had come down from the corries before Sheumas rose to go. He said he was not returning to Alltnalee, but was going upon the hill, for a big herd of deer had come over the ridge of Mel Mòr. Sheumas, though skilled in all hill and forest craft, was not a sure shot, as was his kinsman and my host, Alasdair McIan.

"You will need help," I remember Alasdair Ardoch saying mockingly, adding, "Co dhiubh is fhearr let mise thoir sealladh na fàileadh dhiubh?"—that is to say, Whether would you rather me to deprive them of sight or smell?

This is a familiar saying among the old sportsmen in my country, where it is believed that a few favoured individuals have the power to deprive deer of either sight or smell, as the occasion suggests.

"Dhuit ciàr nan carn!—The gloom of the rocks be upon you!" replied Sheumas, sullenly; "mayhap the hour is come when the red stag will sniff at my nostrils."

With that dark saying he went. None of us saw him again alive.

Was it a forewarning? I have often wondered. Or had he sight of the shadow?

It was three days after this, and shortly after sunrise, that, on crossing the south slope of Mel Mòr with Alasdair Ardoch, we came suddenly upon the body of Sheumas, half submerged in a purple billow of heather. It did not, at the moment, occur to me that he was dead. I had not known that his prolonged absence had been noted, or that he had been searched for. As a matter of fact, he must have died immediately before our approach, for his limbs were still loose, and he lay as a sleeper lies.

Alasdair kneeled and raised his kinsman's head. When it lay upon the purple tussock, the warmth and glow from the sunlit ling gave a fugitive deceptive light to the pale face. I know not whether the sun can have any chemic action upon the dead. But it seemed to me that a dream rose to the face of Sheumas, like one of those submarine flowers that are said to rise at times and be visible for a moment in the hollow of a wave. The dream, the light, waned; and there was a great stillness and white peace where the trouble had been. "It is the Smoothing of the Hand," said Alasdair McIan, in a hushed voice.

Often I had heard this lovely phrase in the Western Isles, but always as applied to sleep. When a fretful child suddenly falls into quietude and deep slumber, an isles-woman will say that it is because of the Smoothing of the Hand. It is always a profound sleep, and there are some who hold it almost as a sacred thing, and never to be disturbed.

So, thinking only of this, I whispered to my friend to come away; that Sheumas was dead weary with hunting upon the hills; that he would awake in due time.

McIan looked at me, hesitated, and said nothing. I saw him glance around. A few yards away, beside a great boulder in the heather, a small rowan stood, flickering its feather-like shadows across the white wool of a ewe resting underneath. He moved thitherward slowly, plucked a branch heavy with scarlet berries, and then, having returned, laid it across the breast of his kinsman.

I knew now what was that passing of the trouble in the face of Sheumas Dhu, what that sudden light was, that calming of the sea, that ineffable quietude. It was the Smoothing of the Hand.

THE ANOINTED MAN

This story is one of the Achanna series (see "The Dàn-nan-Ròn" and "Green Branches" in Vol. III., "Tragic Romances"). See also the note to these two tales, apposite to the use of the forename Gloom and the surname Achanna.

The forename Alison is properly a woman's name, but is occasionally given to a male child—whence, no doubt, the not infrequent occurrence of 'Alison' as a surname.

Of the seven Achannas—sons of Robert Achanna of Achanna in Galloway, self-exiled in the far north because of a bitter feud with his kindred—who lived upon Eilanmore in the Summer Isles, there was not one who was not, in more or less degree, or at some time or other, fëy.

Doubtless I shall have occasion to allude to one and all again, and certainly to the eldest and youngest: for they were the strangest folk I have known or met anywhere in the Celtic lands, from the sea-pastures of the Solway to the kelp-strewn beaches of Lewis. Upon James, the seventh son, the doom of his people fell last and most heavily. Some day I may tell the full story of his strange life and tragic undoing, and of his piteous end. As it happened, I knew best the eldest and youngest of the brothers, Alison and James. Of the others, Robert, Allan, William, Marcus, and Gloom, none save the last-named survives, if peradventure he does, or has been seen of man for many years past. Of Gloom (strange and unaccountable name, which used to terrify me—the more so as, by the savagery of fate, it was the name of all names suitable for Robert Achanna's sixth son) I know nothing beyond the fact that, ten years or more ago, he was a Jesuit priest in Rome, a bird of passage, whence come and whither bound no inquiries of mine could discover. Two years ago a relative told me that Gloom was dead; that he had been slain by some Mexican noble in an old city of Hispaniola, beyond the seas. Doubtless the news was founded on truth, though I have ever a vague unrest when I think of Gloom; as though he were travelling hitherward, as though his feet, on some urgent errand, were already white with the dust of the road that leads to my house.

But now I wish to speak only of Alison Achanna. He was a friend whom I loved, though he was a man of close on forty and I a girl less than half his years. We had much in common, and I never knew anyone more companionable, for all that he was called "Silent Ally." He was tall, gaunt, loosely-built. His eyes were of that misty blue which smoke takes when it rises in the woods. I used to think them like the tarns that lay amid the canna and gale-surrounded swamps in Uist, where I was wont to dream as a child.

I had often noticed the light on his face when he smiled—a light of such serene joy as young mothers have sometimes over the cradles of their firstborn. But for some reason I had never wondered about it, not even when I heard and dimly understood the half-contemptuous, half-reverent mockery with which, not only Alison's brothers, but even his father, at times used towards him. Once, I remember, I was puzzled when, on a bleak day in a stormy August, I overheard Gloom say, angrily and scoffingly, "There goes the Anointed Man!" I looked, but all I could see was that, despite the dreary cold, despite the ruined harvest, despite the rotting potato-crop, Alison walked slowly onward, smiling, and with glad eyes brooding upon the grey lands around and beyond him.

It was nearly a year thereafter—I remember the date, because it was that of my last visit to Eilanmore—that I understood more fully. I was walking westward with Alison towards sundown. The light was upon his face as though it came from within; and when I looked again, half in awe, I saw that there was no glamour out of the west, for the evening was dull and threatening rain. He was in sorrow. Three months before, his brothers Allan and William had been drowned; a month later, his brother Robert had sickened, and now sat in the ingle from morning till the covering of the peats, a skeleton almost, shivering, and morosely silent, with large staring eyes. On the large bed in the room above the kitchen old Robert Achanna lay, stricken with paralysis. It would have been unendurable for me but for Alison and James, and, above all, for my loved girl-friend, Anne Gillespie, Achanna's niece, and the sunshine of his gloomy household.

As I walked with Alison I was conscious of a well-nigh intolerable depression. The house we had left was so mournful; the bleak sodden pastures were so mournful; so mournful was the stony place we were crossing, silent but for the thin crying of the curlews; and, above all, so mournful was the sound of the ocean as, unseen, it moved sobbingly round the isle: so beyond words distressing was all this to me, that I stopped abruptly, meaning to go no farther, but to return to the house, where at least there was warmth, and where Anne would sing for me as she spun.

But when I looked up into my companion's face I saw in truth the light that shone from within. His eyes were upon a forbidding stretch of ground, where the blighted potatoes rotted among a wilderness of round skull-white stones. I remember them still, these strange far-blue eyes, lamps of quiet joy, lamps of peace they seemed to me.

"Are you looking at Achnacarn?" (as the tract was called), I asked, in what I am sure was a whisper.

"Yes," replied Alison slowly; "I am looking. It is beautiful—beautiful. O God, how beautiful is this lovely world!"

I know not what made me act so, but I threw myself on a heathery ridge close by, and broke out into convulsive sobbings.

Alison stooped, lifted me in his strong arms, and soothed me with soft, caressing touches and quieting words.

"Tell me, my fawn, what is it? What is the trouble?" he asked again and again.

"It is you—it is you, Alison," I managed to say coherently at last. "It terrifies me to hear you speak as you did a little ago. You must be fëy. Why—why do you call that hateful, hideous field beautiful on this dreary day—and—and after all that has happened,—O Alison?"

At this, I remember, he took his plaid and put it upon the wet heather, and then drew me thither, and seated himself and me beside him.

"Is it not beautiful, my fawn?" he asked, with tears in his eyes. Then, without waiting for my answer, he said quietly, "Listen, dear, and I will tell you."

He was strangely still—breathless, he seemed to me—for a minute or more. Then he spoke.

"I was little more than a child—a boy just in my teens—when something happened, something that came down the Rainbow-Arches of Cathair-Sìth." He paused here, perhaps to see if I followed, which I did, familiar as I was with all fairy-lore. "I was out upon the heather, in the time when the honey oozes in the bells and cups. I had always loved the island and the sea. Perhaps I was foolish, but I was so glad with my joy that golden day that I threw myself on the ground and kissed the hot, sweet ling, and put my hands and arms into it, sobbing the while with my vague, strange yearning. At last I lay still, nerveless, with my eyes closed. Suddenly I was aware that two tiny hands had come up through the spires of the heather, and were pressing something soft and fragrant upon my eyelids. When I opened them, I could see nothing unfamiliar. No one was visible. But I heard a whisper: 'Arise and go away from this place at once; and this night do not venture out, lest evil befall you.' So I rose, trembling, and went home. Thereafter I was the same, and yet not the same. Never could I see as they saw, what my father and brothers or the isle-folk looked upon as ugly or dreary. My father was wroth me many times, and called me a fool. Whenever my eyes fell upon those waste and desolated spots, they seemed to me passing fair, radiant with lovely light. At last my father grew so bitter that, mocking me the while, he bade me go to the towns and see there the squalor and sordid hideousness wherein men dwelled. But thus it was with me: in the places they call slums, and among the smoke of factories and the grime of destitution, I could see all that other men saw, only as vanishing shadows. What I saw was lovely, beautiful with strange glory, and the faces of men and women were sweet and pure, and their souls were white. So, weary and bewildered with my unwilling quest, I came back to Eilanmore. And on the day of my home-coming, Morag was there—Morag of the Falls. She turned to my father and called him blind and foolish. 'He has the white light upon his brows,' she said of me; 'I can see it, like the flicker-light in a wave when the wind's from the south in thunder-weather. He has been touched with the Fairy Ointment. The Guid Folk know him. It will be thus with him till the day of his death, if a duinshee can die, being already a man dead yet born anew. He upon whom the Fairy Ointment has been laid must see all that is ugly and hideous and dreary and bitter through a glamour of beauty. Thus it hath been since the Mhic-Alpine ruled from sea to sea, and thus is it with the man Alison your son.'

"That is all, my fawn; and that is why my brothers, when they are angry, sometimes call me the Anointed Man."

"That is all." Yes, perhaps. But oh, Alison Achanna, how often have I thought of that most precious treasure you found in the heather, when the bells were sweet with honey-ooze! Did the wild bees know of it? Would that I could hear the soft hum of their gauzy wings.

Who of us would not barter the best of all our possessions—and some there are who would surrender all—to have one touch laid upon the eyelids—one touch of the Fairy Ointment? But the place is far, and the hour is hidden. No man may seek that for which there can be no quest.

Only the wild bees know of it; but I think they must be the bees of Magh-Mell. And there no man that liveth may wayfare—yet.

THE HILLS OF RUEL

One night Eilidh and Isla and I were sitting before a fire, of pine logs blazing upon peats, and listening to the snow as it whispered against the walls of the house. The wind crying in the glen, and the tumult of the hill-stream in spate, were behind the white confused rumour of the snow.

Eilidh was singing low to herself, and Isla was watching her. I could not look long at him, because of the welling upward of the tears that were in my heart. I know not why they were there.

At last, after a pause wherein each sat intent listening to the disarray without, Eilidh's sweet thrilling voice slid through the silence—

"Over the hills and far away,"

That is the tune I heard one day.

Oh that I too might hear the cruel

Honey-sweet folk of the Hills of Ruel.

I saw a shadow go into Isla's eyes. So I stirred and spoke to my cousin.

"You, Isla, who were born on the Hills of Ruel, should sure have seen something of the honey-sweet folk, as they are called in Eilidh's song."

He did not answer straightway, and I saw Eilidh furtively glance at him.

"I will tell you a story," he said at last simply.

Long, long ago there was a beautiful woman, and her name was Etain, and she was loved by a man. I am not for remembering the name of that man, for it is a story of the far-off days: but he was a prince. I will call him Art, and mayhap he was a son of that Art the Solitary who was wont to hear the songs of the hidden people and to see the moonshine dancers.

This Art loved Etain, and she him. So one day he took her to his dûn, and she was his wife. But, and this was an ill thing for one like Art, who was a poet and dreamer, he loved this woman overmuch. She held his life in the hollow of her hand. Nevertheless, and in her own way, she loved him truly: and for him, blind with the Dream against his eyes, all might have been well, but for one thing. For Art, who was no coward, feared one hazard, and that was death: not his own death, and not even the death of Etain, but death. He loved Etain beyond the narrow frontiers of life: and at that indrawing shadow he stood appalled.

One day, when his longing was great upon him, he went out alone upon the Hills of Ruel. There a man met him, a stranger, comely beyond all men he had seen, with dark eyes of dream, and a shadowy smile.

"And so," he said, "and so, Art the Dreamer, thou art eager to know what way thou mayest meet Etain, in that hour when the shadow of the Shadow is upon thee?"

"Even so; though I know neither thee nor the way by which my name is known unto thee."

"Oh, for sure I am only a wandering singer. But, now that we are met, I will sing to you, Art my lord."

Art looked at him frowningly. This man who called him lord spake with heedless sovereignty.

Then, of a sudden, song eddied off the lips of the man, the air of it marvellous light and of a haunting strangeness: and the words were those that Eilidh there sang by the fire.

Through the dusk of silence which that song made in his brain, Art saw the stranger draw from the fawnskin, slung round his shoulders and held by a gold torque, a reed. The man played upon it.

While he played, there was a stirring on the Hills of Ruel. All the green folk were there. They sang.

Art listened to their honey-sweet song, and grew drowsy with the joy and peace of it. And one there was who sang of deathless life; and Art, murmuring the name of Etain, fell asleep.

He was an old, old man when he awoke, and the grey hair that lay down the side of his face was damp with unremembered tears. But, not knowing this, he rose and cried "Etain," "Etain!"

When he reached his dûn there was no Etain there. He sat down by old ashes, where the wind blew through a chink, and pondered. An old man entered at dusk.

"Where is Etain?" Art asked.

"Etain, the wife of Midir?"

"No; Etain, the wife of Art."

The old man mumbled through his open jaws:

"All these years since I was young, Etain the wife of Art has been Etain the wife of Midir."

"And who is Midir?"

"Midir is the King of the World; he, they say, who makes sand of women's hearts and dust of men's hopes."

"And I have dreamed but an idle dream?" Art cried, with his heart breaking in a sob within him.

"Ay, for if Art you be, you have been dreaming a long dream upon the Hills of Ruel."

But when Art, old now and weak, turned to go back to the honey-sweet folk upon the Hills of Ruel, so that he might dream his dream again, he heard Midir laughing, and he died.

"And that is all," ended Isla abruptly, looking neither at Eilidh nor at me, and staring into the flame of the peats.

But Eilidh smiled no more to herself that night, and no more sang below her breath.

THE FISHER OF MEN

"But now I have grown nothing, being all,

And the whole world weighs down upon my heart."

(Fergus and the Druid.)

When old Sheen nic Lèoid came back to the croft, after she
had been to the burn at the edge of the green airidh, where
she had washed the claar that was for the potatoes at the
peeling, she sat down before the peats.

She was white with years. The mountain wind was chill,
too, for all that the sun had shone throughout the
midsummer day. It was well to sit before the peat-fire.

The croft was on the slope of a mountain and had the south
upon it. North, south, east, and west, other great slopes
reached upward like hollow green waves frozen into
silence by the very wind that curved them so, and freaked
their crests into peaks and jagged pinnacles. Stillness was
in that place for ever and ever. What though the Gorromalt
Water foamed down Ben Nair, where the croft was, and
made a hoarse voice for aye surrendering sound to silence?
What though at times the stones fell from the ridges of Ben
Chaisteal and Maolmòr, and clattered down the barren
declivities till they were slung in the tangled meshes of
whin and juniper? What though on stormy dawns the eagle
screamed as he fought against the wind that graved a thin
line upon the aged front of Ben Mulad, where his eyrie
was: or that the kestrel cried above the rabbit-burrows in

the strath: or that the hill-fox barked, or that the curlew wailed, or that the scattered sheep made an endless mournful crying? What were these but the ministers of silence?

There was no blue smoke in the strath except from the one turf cot. In the hidden valley beyond Ben Nair there was a hamlet, and nigh upon three-score folk lived there; but that was over three miles away. Sheen Macleod was alone in that solitary place, save for her son Alasdair Mòr Og. "Young Alasdair" he was still, though the grey feet of fifty years had marked his hair. Alasdair Og he was while Alasdair Ruadh mac Chalum mhic Lèoid, that was his father, lived. But when Alasdair Ruadh changed, and Sheen was left a mourning woman, he that was their son was Alasdair Og still.

She had sore weariness that day. For all that, it was not the weight of the burden that made her go in and out of the afternoon sun, and sit by the red glow of the peats, brooding deep.

When, nigh upon an hour later, Alasdair came up the slope, and led the kye to the byre, she did not hear him: nor had she sight of him, when his shadow flickered in before him and lay along the floor.

"Poor old woman," he said to himself, bending his head because of the big height that was his, and he there so heavy and strong, and tender, too, for all the tangled black beard and the wild hill-eyes that looked out under bristling grey-black eyebrows.

"Poor old woman, and she with the tired heart that she has. Ay, ay, for sure the weeks lap up her shadow, as the sayin' is. She will be thinking of him that is gone. Ay, or maybe the old thoughts of her are goin' back on their own steps, down this glen an' over that hill an' away beyont that strath, an' this corrie an' that moor. Well, well, it is a good love, that of the mother. Sure a bitter pain it will be to me when there's no old grey hair there to stroke. It's quiet here, terrible quiet, God knows, to Himself be the blessin' for this an' for that; but when she has the white sleep at last, then it'll be a sore day for me, an' one that I will not be able to bear to hear the sheep callin', callin', callin' through the rain on the hills here, and Gorromalt Water an' no other voice to be with me on that day of the days."

She heard a faint sigh, and stirred a moment, but did not look round.

"Muim'-à-ghraidh, is it tired you are, an' this so fine a time, too?"

With a quick gesture, the old woman glanced at him.

"Ah, child, is that you indeed? Well, I am glad of that, for I have the trouble again."

"What trouble, Muim' ghaolaiche?"

But the old woman did not answer. Wearily she turned her face to the peat-glow again.

Alasdair seated himself on the big wooden chair to her right. For a time he stayed silent thus, staring into the red heart of the peats. What was the gloom upon the old heart that he loved? What trouble was it?

At last he rose and put meal and water into the iron pot, and stirred the porridge while it seethed and sputtered. Then he poured boiling water upon the tea in the brown jenny, and put the new bread and the sweet-milk scones on the rude deal board that was the table.

"Come, dear tired old heart," he said, "and let us give thanks to the Being."

"Blessings and thanks," she said, and turned round.

Alasdair poured out the porridge, and watched the steam rise. Then he sat down, with a knife in one hand and the brown-white loaf in the other.

"O God," he said, in the low voice he had in the kirk when the Bread and Wine were given—"O God, be giving us now thy blessing, and have the thanks. And give us peace."

Peace there was in the sorrowful old eyes of the mother. The two ate in silence. The big clock that was by the bed tick-tacked, tick-tacked. A faint sputtering came out of a peat that had bog-gas in it. Shadows moved in the silence, and met and whispered and moved into deep, warm darkness. There was peace.

There was still a red flush above the hills in the west when the mother and son sat in the ingle again.

"What is it, mother-my-heart?" Alasdair asked at last, putting his great red hand upon the woman's knee.

She looked at him for a moment. When she spoke she turned away her gaze again.

"Foxes have holes, and the fowls of the air have their places of rest, but the Son of Man hath not where to lay his head."

"And what then, dear? Sure, it is the deep meaning you have in that grey old head that I'm loving so."

"Ay, lennav-aghray, there is meaning to my words. It is old I am, and the hour of my hours is near. I heard a voice outside the window last night. It is a voice I will not be hearing, no, not for seventy years. It was cradle-sweet, it was."

She paused, and there was silence for a time.

"Well, dear," she began again, wearily, and in a low, weak voice, "it is more tired and more tired I am every day now this last month. Two Sabbaths ago I woke, and there were bells in the air: and you are for knowing well, Alasdair, that no kirk-bells ever rang in Strath-Nair. At edge o' dark on Friday, and by the same token the thirteenth day it was, I fell asleep, and dreamed the mools were on my breast, and that the roots of the white daisies were in the hollows where the eyes were that loved you, Alasdair, my son."

The man looked at her with troubled gaze. No words would come. Of what avail to speak when there is nothing to be said? God sends the gloom upon the cloud, and there is rain: God sends the gloom upon the hill, and there is mist: God sends the gloom upon the sun, and there is winter. It is God, too, sends the gloom upon the soul, and there is change. The swallow knows when to lift up her wing overagainst the shadow that creeps out of the north: the wild swan knows when the smell of snow is behind the sun: the salmon, lone in the brown pool among the hills, hears the deep sea, and his tongue pants for salt, and his fins quiver, and he knows that his time is come, and that the sea calls. The doe knows when the fawn hath not yet quaked in her belly: is not the violet more deep in the shadowy dewy eyes? The woman knows when the babe hath not yet stirred a little hand: is not the wild-rose on her cheek more often seen, and are not the shy tears moist on quiet hands in the dusk? How, then, shall the soul not know when the change is nigh at last? Is it a less thing than a reed, which sees the yellow birch-gold adrift on the lake, and the gown of the heather grow russet when the purple has passed into the sky, and the white bog-down wave grey and tattered where the loneroid grows dark and pungent—which sees, and knows that the breath of the Death-Weaver at the Pole is fast faring along the frozen norland peaks. It is more than a reed, it is more than a wild doe on the hills, it is more than a swallow lifting her wing against the coming of the shadow, it is more than a swan drunken with the savour of the blue wine of the waves when the green Arctic lawns are white and still. It is more than these, which has the Son of God for brother, and is clothed with light. God doth not extinguish at the dark tomb what he hath litten in the dark womb.

Who shall say that the soul knows not when the bird is aweary of the nest, and the nest is aweary of the wind? Who shall say that all portents are vain imaginings? A whirling straw upon the road is but a whirling straw: yet the wind is upon the cheek almost ere it is gone.

It was not for Alasdair Òg, then, to put a word upon the saying of the woman that was his mother, and was age-white, and could see with the seeing of old wise eyes.

So all that was upon his lips was a sigh, and the poor prayer that is only a breath out of the heart.

"You will be telling me, grey sweetheart," he said lovingly, at last—"you will be telling me what was behind the word that you said: that about the foxes that have holes for the hiding, poor beasts, and the birdeens wi' their nests, though the Son o' Man hath not where to lay his head?"

"Ay, Alasdair, my son that I bore long syne an' that I'm leaving soon, I will be for telling you that thing, an' now too, for I am knowing what is in the dark this night o' the nights."

Old Sheen put her head back wearily on the chair, and let her hands lie, long and white, palm-downward upon her knees. The peat-glow warmed the dull grey that lurked under her closed eyes and about her mouth, and in the furrowed cheeks. Alasdair moved nearer and took her right hand in his, where it lay like a tired sheep between two scarped rocks. Gently he smoothed her hand, and wondered why so frail and slight a creature as this small old wizened woman could have mothered a great swarthy man like himself—he a man now, with his two score and ten years, and yet but a boy there at the dear side of her.

"It was this way, Alasdair-mochree," she went on in her low thin voice—like a wind-worn leaf, the man that was her son thought. "It was this way. I went down to the burn to wash the claar, and when I was there I saw a wounded fawn in the bracken. The big sad eyes of it were like those of Maisie, poor lass, when she had the birthing that was her going-call. I went through the bracken, and down by the Gorromalt, and into the Shadowy Glen.

"And when I was there, and standing by the running water, I saw a man by the stream-side. He was tall, but spare and weary: and the clothes upon him were poor and worn. He had sorrow. When he lifted his head at me, I saw the tears. Dark, wonderful, sweet eyes they were. His face was pale. It was not the face of a man of the hills. There was no red in it, and the eyes looked in upon themselves. He was a fair man, with the white hands that a woman has, a woman like the Bantighearna of Glenchaisteal over yonder. His voice, too, was a voice like that: in the softness, and the sweet, quiet sorrow, I am meaning.

"The word that I gave him was in the English: for I thought he was like a man out of Sasunn, or of the southlands somewhere. But he answered me in the Gaelic: sweet, good Gaelic like that of the Bioball over there, to Himself be the praise.

"'And is it the way down the Strath you are seeking,' I asked: 'and will you not be coming up to the house yonder, poor cot though it is, and have a sup of milk, and a rest if it's weary you are?'

"'You are having my thanks for that,' he said, 'and it is as though I had both the good rest and the cool sweet drink. But I am following the flowing water here.'

"'Is it for the fishing?' I asked.

"'I am a Fisher,' he said, and the voice of him was low and sad.

"He had no hat on his head, and the light that streamed through a rowan-tree was in his long hair. He had the pity of the poor in his sorrowful grey eyes.

"'And will you not sleep with us?' I asked again: 'that is, if you have no place to go to, and are a stranger in this country, as I am thinking you are; for I have never had sight of you in the home-straths before.'

"'I am a stranger,' he said, 'and I have no home, and my father's house is a great way off.'

"'Do not tell me, poor man,' I said gently, for fear of the pain, 'do not tell me if you would fain not; but it is glad I will be if you will give me the name you have.'

"'My name is Mac-an-t'-Saoir,' he answered with the quiet deep gaze that was his. And with that he bowed his head, and went on his way, brooding deep.

"Well, it was with a heavy heart I turned, and went back through the bracken. A heavy heart, for sure, and yet, oh peace too, cool dews of peace. And the fawn was there: healed, Alasdair, healed, and whinny-bleating for its doe, that stood on a rock wi' lifted hoof an' stared down the glen to where the Fisher was.

"When I was at the burnside, a woman came down the brae. She was fair to see, but the tears were upon her.

"'Oh,' she cried, 'have you seen a man going this way?'

"'Ay, for sure,' I answered, 'but what man would he be?'

"'He is called Mac-an-t'-Saoir.'

"'Well, there are many men that are called Son of the Carpenter. What will his own name be?'

"'Iosa,' she said.

"And when I looked at her, she was weaving the wavy branches of a thorn near by, and sobbing low, and it was like a wreath or crown that she made.

"'And who will you be, poor woman?' I asked.

"'O my Son, my Son,' she said, and put her apron over her head and went down into the Shadowy Glen, she weeping sore, too, at that, poor woman.

"So now, Alasdair, my son, tell me what thought you have about this thing that I have told you. For I know well whom I met on the brae there, and who the Fisher was. And when I was at the peats here once more I sat down, and my mind sank into myself. And it is knowing the knowledge I am."

"Well, well, dear, it is sore tired you are. Have rest now. But sure there are many men called Macintyre."

"Ay, an' what Gael that you know will be for giving you his surname like that."

Alasdair had no word for that. He rose to put some more peats on the fire. When he had done this, he gave a cry.

The whiteness that was on the mother's hair was now in the face. There was no blood there, or in the drawn lips. The light in the old, dim eyes was like water after frost.

He took her hand in his. Clay-cold it was. He let it go, and it fell straight by the chair, stiff as the cromak he carried when he was with the sheep.

"Oh my God and my God," he whispered, white with the awe, and the bitter cruel pain.

Then it was that he heard a knocking at the door.

"Who is there?" he cried hoarsely.

"Open, and let me in." It was a low, sweet voice, but was that grey hour the time for a welcome?

"Go, but go in peace, whoever you are. There is death here."

"Open, and let me in."

At that, Alasdair, shaking like a reed in the wind, unclasped the latch. A tall fair man, ill-clad and weary, pale, too, and with dreaming eyes, came in.

"Beannachd Dhe an Tigh," he said, "God's blessing on this house, and on all here."

"The same upon yourself," Alasdair said, with the weary pain in his voice. "And who will you be? and forgive the asking."

"I am called Mac-an-t'-Saoir, and Iosa is the name I bear— Jesus, the Son of the Carpenter."

"It is a good name. And is it good you are seeking this night?"

"I am a Fisher."

"Well, that's here an' that's there. But will you go to the Strath over the hill, and tell the good man that is there, the minister, Lachlan MacLachlan, that old Sheen nic Lèoid, wife of Alasdair Ruadh, is dead."

"I know that, Alasdair Òg."

"And how will you be knowing that, and my name too, you that are called Macintyre?"

"I met the white soul of Sheen as it went down by the Shadowy Glen a brief while ago. She was singing a glad song, she was. She had green youth in her eyes. And a man was holding her by the hand. It was Alasdair Ruadh."

At that Alasdair fell on his knees. When he looked up there was no one there. Through the darkness outside the door, he saw a star shining white, and leaping like a pulse.

It was three days after that day of shadow that Sheen Macleod was put under the green turf.

On each night, Alasdair Òg walked in the Shadowy Glen, and there he saw a man fishing, though ever afar off. Stooping he was, always, and like a shadow at times. But he was the man that was called Iosa Mac-an-t'-Saoir— Jesus, the Son of the Carpenter.

And on the night of the earthing he saw the Fisher close by.

"Lord God," he said, with the hush on his voice, and deep awe in his wondering eyes: "Lord God!"

And the Man looked at him.

"Night and day, Alasdair MacAlasdair," he said, "night and day I fish in the waters of the world. And these waters are the waters of grief, and the waters of sorrow, and the waters of despair. And it is the souls of the living I fish for. And lo, I say this thing unto you, for you shall not see me again: Go in peace. Go in peace, good soul of a poor man, for thou hast seen the Fisher of Men."

THE LAST SUPPER

"... and there shall be

Beautiful things made new...."

(Hyperion.)

The last time that the Fisher of Men was seen in Strath-Nair was not of Alasdair Macleod but of the little child, Art Macarthur, him that was born of the woman Mary Gilchrist, that had known the sorrow of women.

He was a little child, indeed, when, because of his loneliness and having lost his way, he lay sobbing among the bracken by the stream-side in the Shadowy Glen.

When he was a man, and had reached the gloaming of his years, he was loved of men and women, for his songs are many and sweet, and his heart was true, and he was a good man and had no evil against any one.

It is he who saw the Fisher of Men when he was but a little lad: and some say that it was on the eve of the day that Alasdair Òg died, though of this I know nothing. And what he saw, and what he heard, was a moonbeam that fell into the dark sea of his mind, and sank therein, and filled it with light for all the days of his life. A moonlit mind was that of Art Macarthur: him that is known best as Ian Mòr, Ian Mòr of the Hills, though why he took the name of Ian Cameron is known to none now but one person, and that need not be for the telling here. He had music always in his mind. I asked him once why he heard what so few heard, but he smiled and said only: "When the heart is full of love, cool dews of peace rise from it and fall upon the mind: and that is when the song of Joy is heard."

It must have been because of this shining of his soul that some who loved him thought of him as one illumined. His mind was a shell that held the haunting echo of the deep seas: and to know him was to catch a breath of the infinite ocean of wonder and mystery and beauty of which he was the quiet oracle. He has peace now, where he lies under the heather upon a hillside far away: but the Fisher of Men will send him hitherward again, to put a light upon the wave and a gleam upon the brown earth.

I will tell this sgeul as Ian Mòr that was the little child Art Macarthur, told it to me.

Often and often it is to me all as a dream that comes unawares. Often and often have I striven to see into the green glens of the mind whence it comes, and whither, in a flash, in a rainbow gleam, it vanishes. When I seek to draw close to it, to know whether it is a winged glory out of the soul, or was indeed a thing that happened to me in my tender years, lo—it is a dawn drowned in day, a star lost in the sun, the falling of dew.

But I will not be forgetting: no, never: no, not till the silence of the grass is over my eyes: I will not be forgetting that gloaming.

Bitter tears are those that children have. All that we say with vain words is said by them in this welling spray of pain. I had the sorrow that day. Strange hostilities lurked in the familiar bracken. The soughing of the wind among the trees, the wash of the brown water by my side, that had been companionable, were voices of awe. The quiet light upon the grass flamed.

The fierce people that lurked in shadow had eyes for my helplessness. When the dark came I thought I should be dead, devoured of I knew not what wild creature. Would mother never come, never come with saving arms, with eyes like soft candles of home?

Then my sobs grew still, for I heard a step. With dread upon me, poor wee lad that I was, I looked to see who came out of the wilderness. It was a man, tall and thin and worn, with long hair hanging adown his face. Pale he was as a moonlit cot on the dark moor, and his voice was low and sweet. When I saw his eyes I had no fear upon me at all. I saw the mother-look in the grey shadow of them.

"And is that you, Art lennavan-mo?" he said, as he stooped and lifted me.

I had no fear. The wet was out of my eyes.

"What is it you will be listening to now, my little lad?" he whispered, as he saw me lean, intent, to catch I know not what.

"Sure," I said, "I am not for knowing: but I thought I heard a music away down there in the wood."

I heard it, for sure. It was a wondrous sweet air, as of one playing the feadan in a dream. Callum Dall, the piper, could give no rarer music than that was; and Callum was a seventh son, and was born in the moonshine.

"Will you come with me this night of the nights, little Art?" the man asked me, with his lips touching my brow and giving me rest.

"That I will indeed and indeed," I said. And then I fell asleep.

When I awoke we were in the huntsman's booth, that is at the far end of the Shadowy Glen.

There was a long rough-hewn table in it, and I stared when I saw bowls and a great jug of milk and a plate heaped with oatcakes, and beside it a brown loaf of rye-bread.

"Little Art," said he who carried me, "are you for knowing now who I am?"

"You are a prince, I'm thinking," was the shy word that came to my mouth.

"Sure, lennav-aghrày, that is so. It is called the Prince of Peace I am."

"And who is to be eating all this?" I asked.

"This is the last supper," the prince said, so low that I could scarce hear; and it seemed to me that he whispered, "For I die daily, and ever ere I die the Twelve break bread with me."

It was then I saw that there were six bowls of porridge on the one side and six on the other.

"What is your name, O prince?"

"Iosa."

"And will you have no other name than that?"

"I am called Iosa mac Dhe."

"And is it living in this house you are?"

"Ay. But Art, my little lad, I will kiss your eyes, and you shall see who sup with me."

And with that the prince that was called Iosa kissed me on the eyes, and I saw.

"You will never be quite blind again," he whispered, and that is why all the long years of my years I have been glad in my soul.

What I saw was a thing strange and wonderful. Twelve men sat at that table, and all had eyes of love upon Iosa. But they were not like any men I had ever seen. Tall and fair and terrible they were, like morning in a desert place; all save one, who was dark, and had a shadow upon him and in his wild eyes.

It seemed to me that each was clad in radiant mist. The eyes of them were as stars through that mist.

And each, before he broke bread, or put spoon to the porridge that was in the bowl before him, laid down upon the table three shuttles.

Long I looked upon that company, but Iosa held me in his arms, and I had no fear.

"Who are these men?" he asked me.

"The Sons of God," I said, I not knowing what I said, for it was but a child I was.

He smiled at that. "Behold," he spoke to the twelve men who sat at the table, "behold the little one is wiser than the wisest of ye." At that all smiled with the gladness and the joy, save one; him that was in the shadow. He looked at me, and I remembered two black lonely tarns upon the hillside, black with the terror because of the kelpie and the drowner.

"Who are these men?" I whispered, with the tremor on me that was come of the awe I had.

"They are the Twelve Weavers, Art, my little child."

"And what is their weaving?"

"They weave for my Father, whose web I am."

At that I looked upon the prince, but I could see no web.

"Are you not Iosa the Prince?"

"I am the Web of Life, Art lennavan-mo."

"And what are the three shuttles that are beside each Weaver?"

I know now that when I turned my child's-eyes upon these shuttles I saw that they were alive and wonderful, and never the same to the seeing.

"They are called Beauty and Wonder and Mystery."

And with that Iosa mac Dhe sat down and talked with the Twelve. All were passing fair, save him who looked sidelong out of dark eyes. I thought each, as I looked at him, more beautiful than any of his fellows; but most I loved to look at the twain who sat on either side of Iosa.

"He will be a Dreamer among men," said the prince; "so tell him who ye are."

Then he who was on the right turned his eyes upon me. I leaned to him, laughing low with the glad pleasure I had because of his eyes and shining hair, and the flame as of the blue sky that was his robe.

"I am the Weaver of Joy," he said. And with that he took his three shuttles that were called Beauty and Wonder and Mystery, and he wove an immortal shape, and it went forth of the room and out into the green world, singing a rapturous sweet song.

Then he that was upon the left of Iosa the Life looked at me, and my heart leaped. He, too, had shining hair, but I could not tell the colour of his eyes for the glory that was in them. "I am the Weaver of Love," he said, "and I sit next the heart of Iosa." And with that he took his three shuttles that were called Beauty and Wonder and Mystery and he wove an immortal shape, and it went forth of the room and into the green world singing a rapturous sweet song.

Even then, child as I was, I wished to look on no other. None could be so passing fair, I thought, as the Weaver of Joy and the Weaver of Love.

But a wondrous sweet voice sang in my ears, and a cool, soft hand laid itself upon my head, and the beautiful lordly one who had spoken said, "I am the Weaver of Death," and the lovely whispering one who had lulled me with rest said, "I am the Weaver of Sleep." And each wove with the shuttles of Beauty and Wonder and Mystery, and I knew not which was the more fair, and Death seemed to me as Love, and in the eyes of Dream I saw Joy.

My gaze was still upon the fair wonderful shapes that went forth from these twain—from the Weaver of Sleep, an immortal shape of star-eyed Silence, and from the Weaver of Death a lovely Dusk with a heart of hidden flame—when I heard the voice of two others of the Twelve. They were like the laughter of the wind in the corn, and like the golden fire upon that corn. And the one said, "I am the Weaver of Passion," and when he spoke I thought that he was both Love and Joy, and Death and Life, and I put out my hands. "It is Strength I give," he said, and he took and kissed me. Then, while Iosa took me again upon his knee, I saw the Weaver of Passion turn to the white glory beside him, him that Iosa whispered to me was the secret of the world, and that was called "The Weaver of Youth." I know not whence nor how it came, but there was a singing of skiey birds when these twain took the shuttles of Beauty and Wonder and Mystery, and wove each an immortal shape, and bade it go forth out of the room into the green world, to sing there for ever and ever in the ears of man a rapturous sweet song.

"O Iosa," I cried, "are these all thy brethren? for each is fair as thee, and all have lit their eyes at the white fire I see now in thy heart."

But, before he spake, the room was filled with music. I trembled with the joy, and in my ears it has lingered ever, nor shall ever go. Then I saw that it was the breathing of the seventh and eighth, of the ninth and the tenth of those star-eyed ministers of Iosa whom he called the Twelve: and the names of them were the Weaver of Laughter, the Weaver of Tears, the Weaver of Prayer, and the Weaver of Peace. Each rose and kissed me there. "We shall be with you to the end, little Art," they said: and I took hold of the hand of one, and cried, "O beautiful one, be likewise with the woman my mother," and there came back to me the whisper of the Weaver of Tears: "I will, unto the end."

Then, wonderingly, I watched him likewise take the shuttles that were ever the same and yet never the same, and weave an immortal shape. And when this Soul of Tears went forth of the room, I thought it was my mother's voice singing that rapturous sweet song, and I cried out to it.

The fair immortal turned and waved to me. "I shall never be far from thee, little Art," it sighed, like summer rain falling on leaves: "but I go now to my home in the heart of women."

There were now but two out of the Twelve. Oh the gladness and the joy when I looked at him who had his eyes fixed on the face of Iosa that was the Life! He lifted the three shuttles of Beauty and Wonder and Mystery, and he wove a Mist of Rainbows in that room; and in the glory I saw that even the dark twelfth one lifted up his eyes and smiled.

"O what will the name of you be?" I cried, straining my arms to the beautiful lordly one. But he did not hear, for he wrought Rainbow after Rainbow out of the mist of glory that he made, and sent each out into the green world, to be for ever before the eyes of men.

"He is the Weaver of Hope," whispered Iosa mac Dhe; "and he is the soul of each that is here."

Then I turned to the twelfth, and said "Who art thou, O lordly one with the shadow in the eyes."

But he answered not, and there was silence in the room. And all there, from the Weaver of Joy to the Weaver of Peace, looked down, and said nought. Only the Weaver of Hope wrought a rainbow, and it drifted into the heart of the lonely Weaver that was twelfth.

"And who will this man be, O Iosa mac Dhe?" I whispered.

"Answer the little child," said Iosa, and his voice was sad.

Then the Weaver answered:

"I am the Weaver of Glory——," he began, but Iosa looked at him, and he said no more.

"Art, little lad," said the Prince of Peace, "he is the one who betrayeth me for ever. He is Judas, the Weaver of Fear."

And at that the sorrowful shadow-eyed man that was the twelfth took up the three shuttles that were before him.

"And what are these, O Judas?" I cried eagerly, for I saw that they were black.

When he answered not, one of the Twelve leaned forward and looked at him. It was the Weaver of Death who did this thing.

"The three shuttles of Judas the Fear-Weaver, O little Art," said the Weaver of Death, "are called Mystery, and Despair, and the Grave."

And with that Judas rose and left the room. But the shape that he had woven went forth with him as his shadow: and each fared out into the dim world, and the Shadow entered into the minds and into the hearts of men, and betrayed Iosa that was the Prince of Peace.

Thereupon, Iosa rose and took me by the hand, and led me out of that room. When, once, I looked back I saw none of the Twelve save only the Weaver of Hope, and he sat singing a wild sweet song that he had learned of the Weaver of Joy, sat singing amid a mist of rainbows and weaving a radiant glory that was dazzling as the sun.

And at that I woke, and was against my mother's heart, and she with the tears upon me, and her lips moving in a prayer.

THE AWAKENING OF ANGUS OGUE

One noon, among the hills, Angus Ogue lay in sleep. It was a fair place where he lay, with the heather about him and the bracken with its September gold in it. On the mountain-slope there was not a juniper tall enough, not a rock big enough, to give poise to a raven: all of gold bracken and purple heather it was, with swards of the paler ling. The one outstanding object was a mountain ash. Midway it grew, and leaned so that when the sun was in the east above Ben Monach, the light streamed through the feather-foliage upon the tarn just beneath: so leaned, that when the sun was on the sea-verge of Ben Mheadhonach in the west, the glow, lifting upward over leagues of yellow bracken, turned the rowan-feathers to the colour of brass, and the rowan-berries into bronze.

The tarn was no more than a boulder-set hollow. It was fed by a spring that had slipped through the closing granite in a dim far-off age, and had never ceased to put its cool lips round the little rocky basin of that heather-pool. At the south end the ling fell over its marge in a curling wave: under the mountain-ash there was a drift of moss and fragrant loneroid, as the Gaels call the bog-myrtle.

Here it was, through the tides of noon, that Angus Ogue slept. The god was a flower there in the sunflood. His hair lay upon the green loneroid, yellow as fallen daffodils in the grass. Above him was the unfathomable sea of blue. Not a cloudlet drifted there, nor the wandering shadow of an eagle soaring from a mountain-eyrie or ascending in wide gyres of flight from invisible lowlands.

Around him there was the same deep peace. Not a breath stirred the rowan-leaves, or the feathery shadows these cast upon his white limbs: not a breath frayed the spires of the heather on the ridges of Ben Monach: not a breath slid along the aërial pathways to where, on Ben Mheadhonach, the sea-wind had fallen in a garth of tansies and moon-daisies, and swooned there is the sun-haze, moveless as a lapsed wave.

Yet there were eyes to see, for Orchil lifted her gaze from where she dreamed her triune dream beneath the heather. The goddess ceased from her weaving at the looms of life and death, and looked broodingly at Angus Ogue—Angus, the fair god, the ever-young, the lord of love, of music, of song.

"Is it time that he slept indeed?" she murmured, after a long while, wherein she felt the sudden blood redden her lips and the pulse in her quiet veins leap like a caged bird.

But while she still pondered this thing, three old Druids came over the shoulder of the hill, and advanced slowly to where the Yellow-haired One lay adream. These, however, she knew to be no mortals, but three of the ancient gods.

When they came upon Angus Ogue they sought to wake him, but Orchil had breathed a breath across a granite rock and blown the deep immemorial age of it upon him, so that even the speech of the elder gods was no more in his ears than a gnat's idle rumour.

"Awake," said Keithoir, and his voice was as the sigh of pine-forests when the winds surge from the pole.

"Awake," said Manannan, and his voice was as the hollow booming of the sea.

"Awake," said Hesus, and his voice was as the rush of the green world through space, or as the leaping of the sun.

But Angus Ogue stirred not, and dreamed only that a mighty eagle soared out of the infinite, and scattered planets and stars as the dust of its pinions: and that as these planets fell they expanded into vast oceans whereon a myriad million waves leaped and danced in the sunlight, singing a laughing song: and that as the stars descended in a silver rain they spread into innumerable forests, wherein went harping the four winds of the world, and amidst which the white doves that were his kisses flitted through the gold and shadow.

"He will awake no more," murmured Keithoir, and the god of the green world moved sorrowfully apart, and played upon a reed the passing sweet song that is to this day in the breath of the wind in the grass, or its rustle in the leaves, or its sigh in the lapping of reedy waters.

"He will awake no more," murmured Manannan, and the god of the dividing seas moved sorrowfully upon his way; and on the hillside there was a floating echo as of the ocean-music in a shell, mournful with ancient mournfulness and the sorrow-song of age upon age. The sound of it is in the ears of the dead, where they move through the glooms of silence: and it haunts the time-worn shores of the dying world.

"He will awake no more," murmured Hesus; and the unseen god, whose pulse is beneath the deepest sea and whose breath is the frosty light of the stars, moved out of the shadow into the light, and was at one with it, so that no eyes beheld the radiance which flowered icily in the firmament and was a flame betwixt the earth and the sun, which was a glory amid the cloudy veils about the west and a gleam where quiet dews sustained the green spires of the grass. And as the light lifted and moved, like a vast tide, there was a rumour as of a starry procession sweeping through space to the clashing cymbals of dead moons, to the trumpetings of volcanic worlds, and to the clarions of a thousand suns. But Angus Ogue had the deep immemorial age of the granite upon him, and he slept as the dead sleep.

Orchil smiled. "They are old, old, the ancient gods," she whispered: "they are so old, they cannot see eternity at rest. For Angus Ogue is the god of Youth, and he only is eternal and unchanging."

Then, before she turned once more to her looms of life and death, she lifted her eyes till her gaze pierced the brown earth and rose above the green world and was a trouble amid the quietudes of the sky. Thereat the icy stars gave forth snow, and Angus Ogue was wrapped in a white shroud that was not as that which melts in the flame of noon. Moreover, Orchil took one of the shadows of oblivion from her mystic loom, and put it as a band around Ben Monach where Angus Ogue lay under the mountain-ash by the tarn.

A thousand years passed, and when for the thousandth time the wet green smell of the larches drifted out of Winter into Spring, Orchil lifted her eyes from where she spun at her looms of life and death. For, over the shoulder of the hill, came three old Druids, advancing slowly to where the Yellow-haired One lay adream beneath the snow.

"Awake, Angus," cried Keithoir.

"Awake, Angus," cried Manannan.

"Awake, Angus," cried Hesus.

"Awake, awake," they cried, "for the world has suddenly grown chill and old."

They had the grey grief upon them, when they stood there, face to face with Silence.

Then Orchil put down the shuttle of mystery wherewith she wove the threads of her looms, and spoke.

"O ye ancient gods, answer me this. Keithoir, if death were to come to thee, what would happen?"

"The green world would wither as a dry leaf, and as a dead leaf be blown idly before the wind that knows not whither it bloweth."

"Manannan, if death were to come to thee, what would happen?"

"The deep seas would run dry, O Orchil: there would be sand falling in the place of the dews, and at last the world would reel and fall into the abyss."

"Hesus, if death were to come to thee, what would happen?"

"There would be no pulse at the heart of earth, O Orchil, no lift of any star against any sun. There would be a darkness and a silence."

Then Orchil laughed.

"And yet," she said, "when Angus Ogue had the snow-sleep of a thousand years, none knew it! For a thousand years the pulse of his heart of love has been the rhythmic beat of the world. For a thousand years the breath of his nostrils has been as the coming of Spring in the human heart. For a thousand years the breath of his life has been warm against the lips of lovers. For a thousand years the memory of these has been sweet against oblivion. Nay, not one hath dreamed of the deep sleep of Angus Ogue."

"Who is he?" cried Keithoir. "Is he older than I, who saw the green earth born?"

"Who is he?" cried Manannan. "Is he older than I, who saw the first waters come forth out of the void?"

"Who is he?" cried Hesus. "Is he older than I, who saw the first comet wander from the starry fold; who saw the moon when it was a flaming sun, and the sun when it was a sevenfold intolerable flame?"

"He is older!" said Orchil. "He is the soul of the gods."

And with that she blew a frith across the palm of her hand, and took away the deep immemorial age of the granite that was upon the Fair God.

"Awake, eternal Spring!" she cried. And Angus awoke, and laughed with joy; and at his laughing the whole green earth was veiled in a snow of blossom.

"Arise, eternal Youth!" she cried. And Angus arose and smiled; and at his smiling the old brown world was clad in dewy green, and everywhere the beauty of the world was sweet against the eyes of young and old, and everywhere the pulse of love leaped in beating hearts.

"Go forth, eternal Hope!" she cried. And Angus Ogue passed away on the sunflood, weaving rainbows as he went, that were fair upon the hills of age and light within the valleys of sorrow, and were everywhere a wild, glad joy.

And that is why, when Orchil weaves dumbly in the dark: and Keithoir is blind, and dreams among remote hills and by unfrequented shores: and Manannan lies heavy with deep sleep, with the oceans of the world like moving shadows above him: and Hesus is grown white and hoar with the frost of waning stars and weary with the burden of new worlds: that is why Angus Ogue, the youthful god, is more ancient than they, and is for ever young. Their period is set. Oblivion is upon the march against their immemorial time. But in the heart of Angus Ogue blooms the Rose of Youth, whose beauty is everlasting. Yea, Time is the name of that rose, and Eternity the beauty and fragrance thereof.

FOOTNOTES

[1]The "leabhar-aifrionn" (pron. lyo-ur eff-runn) is a missal: literally a mass-book, or chapel-book. Bru-dhearg is literally red-breast.

[2]"O my Grief, my Grief."

[3]The first part of the story of Ula and Urla, as Isla and Eilidh, is told in "Silk o' the Kine," at the end of The Sin-Eater. [The name Eilidh, is pronounced Eily (liq.) or Isle-ih.]

[4]Pronounce mogh-rāy, mogh-rēe (my heart's delight—lit. my dear one, my heart).

Printed in Great Britain
by Amazon